FLASHBACK

Books by Helen McKenna

The Beach House Series

The Beach House
The Perfect Proposal (short story)
Third Offence

Other Novels

Room 46

Short Stories

Flashback (includes The Perfect Proposal)

Combined Editions

Room 46 & Short Story Collection

All titles also available as e-books.

FLASHBACK

Helen McKenna

Flashback
By Helen McKenna

Previously published as *The Perfect Proposal And Other Stories* (excluding stories Diamond Pudding and Good Things).

Published by Lightning Source

ISBN 13: 9780648264125

Website: www.helenmckenna.com.au
Email: info@helenmckenna.com.au

CONTENTS

Stalked!... 7

The Group 21

Good Things 37

Pseudo 59

Diamond Pudding 77

The Perfect Proposal.................................. 97

Preview of The Beach House 141

About The Author.. 167

STALKED!

$\mathcal{P}$atience really was a virtue.

He'd been coming down to his special hidey-hole every Thursday for weeks now, but the timing was never right. Either somebody else came along...or she was holding a cup of coffee that could be flung in his face...or she was wearing sneakers which would allow her to run away.

But today - today the planets had aligned in his favour. Not only was she beverage free but she was also wearing stilettos. Ridiculously high, thin heeled stilettos. Her gait was already compromised as she walked along the gravel verge so he knew that once she hit the grass she would be as vulnerable as a fly on sticky paper.

And to top it all off there was not another person in sight.

Shifting slightly forward, he tried to block out the discomfort in his legs from squatting in such an awkward position. Just breathe, he reminded himself. He was as tense as a coiled spring but knew he needed to control himself for just a bit longer. If he pounced now, there was a chance she might keep walking along the road. No, it was better to wait until she was right in his line of sight, in the secluded spot he had especially chosen.

Her hair was up today, which was a shame. He really preferred it long and flowing freely. And the outfit...well, it wasn't one of her best. But hey, you couldn't have it all, right?

His heart started to pound as she approached the

northern end of the park. Just a few more steps and she would finally be his…

*T*he throaty growl of her neighbour's souped up Falcon ute roused Ella from a deep sleep. Annoyed at her slumber being interrupted before the alarm went off, she buried her head under the pillow. It didn't help much. Although muffled, the Falcon's engine kept revving.

Rrrrrr… RRRrrrrr… Rrrrrrr…

Jeez do you have to do that every day, Greg? she fumed. Why can't you just turn on the engine and go?

Finally, after some spectacular gravel spinning and several more revs, the noise eased as Greg drove away.

'Halleluiah!' Ella mumbled. What's he doing leaving so early anyway? she wondered. Greg usually hooned off at five past seven on the dot, by which time she was eating her breakfast and could drown out the revving by turning up the volume on the TV.

It was the unmistakable rumble of the rubbish truck that roused Ella next, just as she was drifting back to sleep.

'What's with everyone running ahead of schedule today?' she thought, plumping her pillow with a savage thump. Was it too much to ask for a little peace at such an uncivilised hour?

Dragging her doona up around her head, Ella wrapped herself in it cosily, determined to at least remain in bed, even if not asleep, until her alarm actually sounded. It was a point of principle for Ella, unlike her housemate, Natalie, who saw no point in lolling in bed if she was awake and could be up doing something.

Thinking of Natalie, she was being surprisingly quiet this morning. A theatre nurse who worked day shift, Natalie usually thought nothing of clattering around the kitchen and bathroom as she prepared for her 6.45am start.

Maybe I'd better go and wake her, Ella thought. But, then again, it's not my job, she reassured herself. Natalie can get herself up and organised. It would actually be kind of funny to see Miss Cool, Calm and Collected in a total spin. Ella smiled at the thought of it.

It wasn't that she didn't like Natalie, they were just *very* different people. And the truth was if they hadn't been thrown together as housemates there was little likelihood they would otherwise be friends.

The realisation finally hit Ella when she heard Greg's wife hurrying their kids to get to the bus stop. Launching herself to a sitting position, she reached over to the bedside table for her mobile phone. Of course it wasn't there; she had put it on the charger in the kitchen last night. That's why her alarm hadn't gone off.

Nooooo!

Wild eyed, she leapt out of bed and grabbed her watch from the dressing table. '7:22!' she exclaimed, calculating that she had exactly fourteen minutes to get out of the house if she was to make the train.

Usually a woman who liked to take her time getting ready, Ella was amazed at the speed she could move when she had to. Following a two-minute shower and a blast of dry shampoo, she coiled her slightly greasy hair into a clamp clip, threw on a polyester dress that didn't require ironing and gulped half a glass of orange juice.

Normally she wouldn't be that concerned about getting to work on time. It wasn't as if Ella loved her job at Brown and Blain Constructions. But it was payroll day and if the system wasn't updated before ten thirty, the pays would be a day late. And a mob of angry construction workers was not something she wanted to contend with.

Sticking her feet into her sneakers for the run to the train station, Ella shoved her work shoes into her oversized handbag and unplugged her phone from the charger. Ignoring the fact it was starting to rain she slammed the door shut behind her and legged it to the train station.

Luckily the train was a few minutes late.

Dragging her GO card over the reader Ella joined the mob boarding the 7.45 City Service and finally slunk aboard just before the doors closed. Hanging onto the handrail, she leant forward for a few moments to catch her breath.

Once recovered, Ella began the long trek to the end carriages. Due to the length of her local platform out in the boondocks, everybody had to embark via the front cars, causing a bottleneck that only subsided when people dispersed through the train.

Finally, she found an empty seat in the second last carriage and slumped onto it, appalled, as always, that she was actually a commuter. How had her life taken this awful turn? Before the GFC Ella had her own apartment in the inner city and earned a substantial income as a PA to an international real estate mogul. Work was a five-minute stroll away, punctuated by a coffee and bagel en route. She'd had a whole extra hour to get ready and would never have been seen dead in her sneakers. Or this dress for that matter, Ella thought glumly. It had been fashionable in its day, but now it looked like something you'd find at Vinnie's, which was exactly where it was going after today, she decided.

Unfortunately, when the US and European real estate markets crashed, so did her career, and much more quickly than she would ever have anticipated. There was no gentle breaking of the bad news and time to gradually wind the business down. Rather Ella was greeted by a security guard one morning, ordered to hand over her phone and laptop and had been given a box of her belongings in return.

At first Ella had remained optimistic, refusing to downsize or branch out into the suburbs. She was a skilled PA who had worked in a multi-million-dollar company, so surely that would hold her in good stead?

As each month passed, however, and no new amazing job offers landed in her lap, Ella had to be practical. With her credit card debt nudging ten grand and on the slippery slope of having to default on her car loan, she finally emerged from the fog of denial. Relying on her rusty secretarial skills, Ella had talked her way into a payroll job in Geebung and curbed her lifestyle to suit.

Selling her car had hurt but not as much as giving up the lease on her apartment. Luckily a friend of a friend had just bought a house way out on the fringe of Brisbane and was looking for a tenant at less than half the rent Ella had previously paid. It had sounded too good to be true and of course it was – in Ella's mind it was simply not possible to be as perpetually positive as Natalie, the commute sucked *and* she had to deal with Natalie's moronic boyfriend Marty – but it was workable, at least in the short term.

Fifteen minutes and a quick make-up job later, Ella felt a bit more human. Slicking some lip gloss on, she checked her reflection in her hand mirror. It'll do for today, she thought, although I really do need to get my roots done.

Kicking off her sneakers, Ella pulled her new Italian sandals out of her bag. Stroking the soft leather, she couldn't help but smile. Yes, they had been ridiculously expensive, and they were impractical for work, but she didn't care. Just because she'd had to downgrade just about everything in her life, it didn't mean she had to completely tame her shoe fetish.

Slipping them on she allowed herself to daydream for a moment. I'm still Ella White, PA extraordinaire, she mused. I spend as much on shoes as some people spend on rent. I eat out just about every night, I get to go on all expenses paid business trips…

The smell of fresh coffee brought her out of her reverie. Ella looked up sharply as a petite young woman in a Cue suit sashayed past, latte held aloft as she chatted into her phone. 'Yeah, that's fine, but just make sure we have enough time for both meetings…'

Cow, thought Ella. How did she manage to keep her corporate career and I didn't? What is she, all of nineteen? Don't get too comfy, sweetie, she thought. You never know what's around the corner.

A little depressed now, she decided to leave her sandals on. Stuff my grubby old sneakers and their comfort, Ella decided, today I am going to arrive in style. Poking her shoes down the edges of her bag, she then reached in deeper to retrieve the dog-eared Cosmo she'd been reading all week.

Ella was engrossed in an article about hair straighteners when the melodic tone of her mobile announced a text message. Reaching down, she felt around absently, her attention still on the article. Finally unearthing the phone, she hit the unlock sequence, missing it twice before it finally co-operated. Stupid phone!

Making the switch from her employer provided iPhone to a no-frills Nokia was a major adjustment Ella still struggled with. She knew she should be grateful that Natalie had managed to swing them a matching pair in a special two for one promotion that included hugely discounted rates when combined with their internet plan but her fun side was still rebelling.

She frowned as the screen flashed "private number". Who outside her address book would be texting her at this time of the morning? Hitting the OK key, the message appeared. It read, "Hey QT I'm watching you."

Ella sat up straighter, her curiosity piqued. Doing her best to look neutral she glanced around the carriage at the familiar faces that made the same journey each day. Nobody appeared to be holding a phone. Before she had time to consider any further the Nokia vibrated in her palm and the message icon appeared. "Love your shoes," it said.

With as little obvious movement as possible she keyed in a reply. "Thanks."

The screen flashed again about 30 seconds later. "Italian?"

"Yeah."

"Running l8 2day?"

Ella glanced around surreptitiously before replying. "Who are you???"

The answer came back in a flash. "An admirer."

"How do you know me?" she typed back.

"I've been watching u for months," said the reply.

"Why not say something?"

"2 shy!"

Thinking for a second, Ella hit the call button and was startled seconds later when a jarring mariachi tune burst into life about five seats in front. Jumping to her feet she followed the sound, amazed to eventually trace it to an elderly woman in a tracksuit.

'Aren't you going to answer that?' Ella demanded.

'What? Oh, is that mine?' the woman asked, opening her bag and rummaging around. Ella glanced at her own phone, only to realise that the call had been rejected already, while the woman's phone was still ringing. Scratch that idea.

The phone vibrated again just as Ella sat back down. "Tricky, tricky!" it read.

"Why didn't you answer?"

"More fun this way."

Ella stared at the screen, frustrated again not to have her iPhone. It could possibly have given her more information. But then again maybe it was more fun this way. She hadn't had a secret admirer since year nine. She could do with a liaison of *some* sort after almost six months of singledom.

"Why me?" she asked.

"You're beautiful."

"Aw shucks."

"I mean it."

"Thx :-)"

For the next five minutes they texted back and forth, each message becoming increasingly flirty.

Finally Ella decided to take control of the situation. "Coffee at Central after work?"

The reply was almost instant. "Maybe".

"Oh, only maybe???"

"I want to REALLY get to know you first."

Ella shook her head. Technology had a lot to answer for sometimes. Guys these days hid behind text messages and emails instead of getting out there and talking to women. As much fun as this had been, she wasn't wasting any more of her phone credit on a loser.

"Sorry, face to face or no chance!"

"We'll see about that!"

At this Ella's stomach clenched. How was she supposed to take that? Was it meant to be funny and friendly or was it a tad threatening? Hitting the lock sequence, she dropped the phone back in her bag and picked up her Cosmo again.

The message beep came almost immediately but Ella didn't respond. Then came another beep and another. Ella knew she shouldn't engage any further but curiosity got the better of her. Checking the screen, her pulse quickened. Each message, accompanied by an angry face, was one word in capitals – DON'T – IGNORE – ME!

Right, thought Ella, you are getting blocked! Holding the phone aloft she scrolled through the menu but couldn't work out how to activate the block function.

The phone beeped again then and although Ella knew it was her imagination, this time the tone seemed menacing.

"Play nice!"

Ella's stomach clenched again, tighter this time. This interaction was getting weird. Shoving the Cosmo into her bag, she got up and walked towards the next carriage, studying each face briefly as she walked past. Dan the nerdy guy from the bank would never try anything so forward. Patrick from Qantas was way too tight with money to send frivolous messages. Reg the park ranger didn't have a mobile phone.

As she stepped into the alcove at the end of the carriage her phone screen lit up again saying, "I know where you live and work."

Ella was starting to feel faint. Recalling the story about mobile phone stalking she had seen on the news the previous week she strode through the next two carriages and sat down next to a woman with a baby. This carriage was much fuller, providing her with a sense of anonymity.

The messages started coming faster then and Ella decided to turn the phone off. As soon as she got to work she would ring the police and have this fruitcake arrested, assuming of course they could trace a private number.

It was only when she turned the phone over to activate the off switch that she noticed the little orange dot on the bottom. The one Natalie had put on *her* phone so they wouldn't get them mixed up.

It's not my phone! Ella realised. Natalie must have picked up the wrong one this morning.

The relief was so immense she almost burst into tears. True, she felt bad for Natalie, but at least she was safe at the hospital for now. She would call the police anyway and then ring Nat and warn her too.

Natalie always claimed she had an inbuilt radar for sensing how genuine a person was within moments of meeting them. Obviously it had short circuited on at least one occasion thought Ella, a tad smugly. She had warned her housemate about being too friendly and trusting of people. Shaking her head, she thought, dear old Nat, living in her little fantasy world. This might just be the shakeup she needed to get with the program and embrace the real world.

Ella bounced off the train at Geebung station, happy to see that the drizzle had dried up and the sun was now shining. It was amazing how your world could be turned upside down and then right side up again in such a short time frame. She actually enjoyed the ten-minute walk to work from the station along the back streets. It was much quieter than along the busy main road and there was a lovely little secluded park where she could sit and catch her breath before facing another day at the coalface.

I really shouldn't have changed my shoes, she berated herself as she sauntered along, these sandals are not made for walking! It's lucky I don't have to run at this end.

Still feeling buoyed by the relief that she wasn't being stalked after all, Ella forgot she wasn't carrying her own phone and didn't even check the screen before answering the phone when it rang as she walked through the deserted park.

'Hello,' she chirped.

The voice was low and menacing. 'Hello, Ella,' the caller said. 'Don't forget to give Natalie back her phone.'

$\mathcal{T}$he timing couldn't have been more perfect.

The call scared Ella so much she dropped the phone and immediately started running, but of course she didn't get far in her shoes.

Emerging from the bushland, he ran over to where she lay crumpled on the ground clasping her left ankle, which was already swelling rapidly. Her handbag and its contents were strewn across the grass nearby. He had never seen her look like this before, scared and helpless. She was usually so poised and controlled. Yet again fate had intervened, amazingly to make him the hero.

At the sight of him she immediately burst into tears.

'Craig!' she exclaimed, between sobs. 'Please help me!'

She knew his name! He thought he was just another employee number to her, a faceless member of the construction crew who visited the payroll office every Thursday morning to sign his timesheet.

Craig had been smitten from the first moment he had laid eyes upon Ella. But he'd always been so shy with women and the office was so crowded that he'd never got the chance to speak to her alone. That was why he had been waiting in hope these past few weeks. What could be more natural than bumping into a workmate and walking with them to the office?

His aim had just been to speak to her, but something much bigger was going on here and he wasn't one to look a gift horse in the mouth.

'Don't cry, Ella,' he soothed, 'everything is going to be all right.'

atalie finally emerged from her room at nine o'clock, sleepy eyed and with crazy bed hair. She wasn't surprised to see Marty ensconced on the couch, watching TV.

'Hey, sleepyhead,' he said, 'Glad you called in sick today?'

'Yeah, what do you reckon?' she replied with a grin. 'I haven't slept in for weeks and I can't wait to catch some rays once we get to Mooloolaba. I'm a big believer in the occasional mental health day.'

'Oh yeah, me too.'

'So, you been here long?' Natalie poured herself a glass of pineapple juice.

'A little while.'

'You weren't bored, were you?'

'No, not a bit, I've been catching up with some text messages.'

'Okay, great. Just give me a minute and we can get going.'

'Sure, Babe, no hurry,' he replied. 'Oh, by the way Ella took your phone by mistake.'

Natalie put her hand over her mouth. 'Oops! That was my fault. It was still half dark when I grabbed it this morning to call work. I didn't realise I got the wrong one.' She raised her right eyebrow questioningly. 'How did you realise that?'

'You left it on the couch. When I picked it up to move it there was no little dot.'

Natalie shook her head. 'Oh no, I feel bad! I hope it doesn't inconvenience Ella too much.'

'No point worrying about it now,' Marty said and then lay down so Natalie wouldn't see his grin.

From the moment she had moved in, Marty had taken an instant dislike to snooty Ella, Miss High and Mighty, who used to have such an important job and a place in the city. He was tired of hearing her whinge about the long commute and how primitive life was out here in the sticks so he had taken the opportunity to make her reconsider her long train journey each morning.

It was fortuitous that he had seen her running down the road with the heel of one of those stupid shoes hanging out of her handbag. Having heard her rave on and on about them they lent a great deal of authenticity to his text conversation. He was also glad he had kept the prepaid SIM card he'd bought on his latest trip to Bali. It was totally untraceable.

Oh yes, he had finally solved the Ella problem.

With a bit of luck, she would be gone before the month was out.

THE GROUP

*B*eth couldn't believe how nervous she was.

It was ridiculous. After all, she was a successful, confident woman with a corporate career. She had two bachelor degrees and an MBA *and* she earned a six-figure salary. Yet, as she stood here in the small, run-down community hall facing a rather motley crew of strangers, her palms were slick with sweat and her heart was pounding as if she'd just leapt off the treadmill.

The pages Beth held in her hands were dog-eared from incessant handling. She had still been flicking between them making last minute adjustments when she was introduced by Gordon and invited up to speak.

Beth couldn't believe how different Gordon was in person. Her impression of him from his emails, and his name, had been an older, distinguished gentleman, and she was still struggling to come to terms with the twenty-something guy with his straggly goatee and waist length ponytail. His face was open and friendly, but also slightly puzzled, as he eyed Beth now, obviously wondering why she hadn't yet spoken.

'Beth?' he prompted.

Beth nodded and managed a weak smile. 'Sorry,' she mumbled, 'I'm just very nervous.'

'No need to be,' Gordon reassured her. 'We were all the newbie once.'

Several other audience members nodded their agreement.

Beth took a deep breath and focused her attention on a spot on the timber-panelled wall. Breathe Beth, she instructed herself. If you can speak at a national conference you can speak here. Yeah, but the national conference was business, she reminded herself, this is personal. You are about to expose a side of yourself that has never been publicly acknowledged.

A woman in the front row coughed and a man up the back glanced at his phone. People fidgeting was not a good sign and Beth knew she had to either get on with it or get out.

Taking another deep breath, she opened her mouth and finally the words began to flow.

*T*he huge thunderclap and accompanying flash of lightening ended Beth's hopes of leaving the office to buy a sandwich and a magazine during her lunchbreak. 'Damn,' she muttered, realising she should have gone half an hour ago. Josie from the secretarial pool had already buzzed twice to remind her that 'lunch hours need to be strictly adhered to so as to ensure the smooth running of Lloyd and Morgan'.

Beth conceded she had a point; after all it was hard to put calls through and schedule appointments when staff didn't stick to their break times. Even so, did everything about the accounting world have to come down to numbers? She had just wanted to get Mrs Borthwick's complex tax return done and *then* enjoy her break.

She clicked on the lodge button and sighed wearily as the file uploaded. It wasn't accounting that was the problem, it was *her*. A box containing her newly updated business cards – which now proudly acknowledged her as Senior Associate – caught her attention. This new position and the pay rise that came with it should make her feel happy, right? A decade of study and hard work had finally been rewarded after all. Yet what she felt now was weighed down with expectation and trapped into a future she didn't want.

The urge inside Beth had been growing stronger for a long time now, it had been there since childhood, really, but she'd never had the courage to tell anybody. In the past she had managed to squash it by working harder and studying more but now as she approached her thirtieth birthday, well, it seemed if she didn't act soon she would go crazy.

Boom!

Another rumble of thunder sounded, followed by the pounding of heavy rain on the roof. Well, that was that, it was the lunchroom or bust today. Flicking her computer to hibernate, Beth picked up her water bottle and trudged down the hall.

Considering that Lloyd and Morgan was a prosperous, long-established firm with very fancy office space, they paid little attention to the state of the staff lunchroom. Stuck in a windowless corner of the building, the fluorescent lighting was much too harsh for the small space and the lingering olfactory reminders of thousands of microwaved meals permeated the room, resulting in a persistent, unpleasant odour. Beth could not understand why more of her colleagues did not choose to escape to a nearby café like she generally did.

Fortunately, the staff club kept a supply of basic food items for sale, so Beth paid one dollar for a packet of generic chicken noodle soup mix and selected a packet of chicken Twisties from the vending machine. After mixing her soup she took a seat at the only vacant table and leafed listlessly through the selection of junk mail, accounting journals and ancient magazines on the table.

Adam, from IT, sat down opposite her, frowning as he examined a bruised Granny Smith apple.

'Whoa,' Beth said, 'that's a lovely looking specimen.'

'Yeah, isn't it just? I found it at the bottom of my backpack and can't quite remember when I put it there,' he admitted. 'But my options are pretty limited, aren't they? I see you snagged the last cup a soup *and* you've hogged all the best reading material.'

'You've got to be quick around here,' Beth laughed. 'But let me save you some time – Coles have a two for one special on tinned tomatoes, Woolies have rolled back the price on Safe toilet paper and according to this extremely ancient *New Idea*, William and Kate are *never* getting married.'

Adam reached over to the next table. 'Here you go,' he smirked, handing her the latest edition of the local community newspaper. 'I'm sure there will be some ground-breaking headlines in here.'

'My humble thanks,' Beth deadpanned. She never read the free paper, but in the absence of anything better today she slid it over and started flicking through it.

It was only a small notice, buried in the free classifieds section, but Beth noticed it immediately. It had occurred to her that a group might be a good outlet, a way to test the waters and try something new without having to turn her whole life upside down.

Maybe it was just what she needed to get the idea out of her system for good. Because, in the end, it *was* a crazy and very impractical desire. She hadn't studied for all those years and worked her butt off for even longer to throw it all away on a whim.

Still, it couldn't hurt to check the group out.

Adam noticed her preoccupation. 'Don't tell me you're getting involved in community affairs.'

'No, nothing that noble. Just checking my stars.'

'Let me guess…you're on the brink of a whole new life cycle *and* destined to meet the man of your dreams?'

'Yeah, something like that.'

'He could be closer than you think,' Adam murmured wistfully.

Beth ignored the comment, having no desire to open *that* particular can of worms today. Waiting until Adam went up to make himself a coffee she tore the page out and tucked it into her bag. She had never believed in fate before but had to admit it was positively providential that she happened to come across that particular advertisement at this particular point in time.

Beth headed back to her desk five minutes early so she could email Gordon the group co-ordinator and was thrilled when a reply pinged back almost immediately.

"Thanks for your interest, Beth," he wrote. "Please find attached information about the group and our meeting schedule for the year. We're a bit of an odd bunch and there are no airs and graces, but we're always on the lookout for new members. Please feel free to email with any questions you may have. Looking forward to meeting you."

"Thanks, Gordon, you too," she replied then conscientiously dragged her attention back to the pile of work on her desk, as unappealing as it was.

Even though the next meeting was still weeks away, Beth immediately found herself in a much better frame of mind at work. How was it that such a seemingly small step towards a dream could buoy up in her the kind of enthusiasm she hadn't felt in years?

Yet at the same time she didn't plan to share her aspirations with any of her workmates. They were all so into accounting in a way that she just wasn't and she knew they could not possibly understand.

Beth almost died when she nearly let it slip at Friday night drinks. Having enjoyed a few wines, she was feeling nicely mellow and got as far as saying, 'I'm joining a...', before pulling herself up.

'Joining a what?' probed Josie, who always took it upon herself to give unsolicited advice on any topic.

'A gym,' she mumbled hoping that the interest would end there.

'Really?' Josie replied excitedly, not seeming to notice she had dropped a clump of salsa down the front of her white blouse. 'I've been thinking about doing that for ages too, let's go together!'

'Uh, yeah, sure,' Beth said, knowing it would probably be forgotten by next week. Josie was notorious for embarking on fitness drives she never followed through with.

Unfortunately this was the one time Josie's motivation was genuine. When Beth arrived at work on Monday morning she found a thick stack of brochures on her desk for all the gyms within a ten-kilometre radius. Logging onto her email, she found a message with an Excel attachment summarising all the information from the brochures.

On Tuesday Josie buttonholed her at morning tea and showed her a series of photographs on her phone. Beth expressed polite interest although she did feel she had to ask why they were all exterior shots of the various gyms in question.

'So you can see what the car parks are like,' Josie explained impatiently. 'It's one of the first things a woman is supposed to check out for safety reasons.'

'Oh, of course.'

On Wednesday, she found a bound document with timetables for various classes arranged in alphabetical order and degree of difficulty.

By Thursday Beth knew she had to speak up. She had no desire to join a gym and it was ridiculous to be forced into it just because Josie was nosey, and because she didn't want her workmates knowing her personal business.

Taking a deep breath, she picked up the phone, then chickened out and started an email instead. "Hey Josie, thanks so much for all the info, particularly the price list you just forwarded. I didn't realise gym memberships were so expensive! I have just realised I really can't afford to join now. Sorry." Just for effect she added a sad face emoji.

Josie's reply was swift and blunt. "You earn more than twice what I do and I can afford it."

Beth stared at the screen but managed to refrain from typing what she really thought, which was something along the lines of "so get your degree, you bossy cow!"

Instead she took the high road and ignored it.

The idea of telling her family her secret was just as unappealing for Beth. To an outsider the professional pedigree of her parents and siblings – lawyers, actuary and systems analyst respectively – was outstanding. How could she risk messing up this perfect picture? It wasn't that she didn't love them, she just knew they would not fathom, or possibly even respect, the choice she was making.

Fortunately it was easy enough to avoid the topic. As always, their weekly Sunday lunch date was full of talk about topics boring enough to lull a hard-core insomniac to sleep within minutes. Well, maybe that was a bit unfair, Beth acknowledged as she poured some more gravy over her roast pork. The rest of her family were technical and analytical and she wasn't – it was as simple as that.

'So, Beth, I guess you're looking ahead to Junior Partner now?' her mother queried.

Beth hesitated a second, but couldn't bring herself to fess up. 'Sure,' she said. 'It's on my five-year plan.'

'Five years?' her brother Nathan scoffed. 'You could do it in three.'

'Yeah, true enough,' she agreed, hugging her secret to herself and smiling inwardly at the thought of where she would actually like to be in three years' time. It certainly wasn't at Lloyd and Morgan.

The next near miss happened the following week. Trapped in

the lunchroom during another summer storm, Beth was half-heartedly listening to the conversation around her when her manager, Camilla, tried to rope her into playing netball in the firm team. 'It's Saturday fortnight at two thirty,' she said, 'And I'll put you as Goal Keeper so it's not too strenuous.'

'Sorry I can't, I've got a meeting,' Beth replied vaguely, as she continued to read her copy of Vogue. She immediately paled when she realised what she'd said.

'What kind of meeting?' demanded Camilla, who saw herself as the star of the netball team and took offence when anybody who was asked to play refused.

Beth had to think on her feet. 'Trust me it's nothing any of you guys would be interested in.'

Adam gave her a sly smile. 'Oh, let me guess, secret women's business, hey?'

'Something like that,' Beth murmured.

'Hmm, sounds intriguing,' Adam teased.

Beth felt like rolling up her magazine and clubbing him with it.

Of course her reply raised many more questions than it answered. The other women at the table continued to look at her with great interest throughout the rest of lunch. Later she heard two of them talking about her in the copy room.

'Well, I'd say it's AA,' Leanne whispered. 'They're not supposed to tell people about it'.

Julia nodded. 'It's always the ones you least suspect. You know I've often seen her looking blankly at things like she's not really there. She's probably got a hip flask somewhere'.

And thus began a surveillance operation to rival ASIO.

Staff began dropping into Beth's office unannounced and appeared disappointed to find her completing tax returns or audits. Conversations stopped when she entered the file room or secretarial pool. Her name was deleted from the email list announcing a new wine club one of the partners was starting.

She even caught Josie smelling the contents of her water bottle.

'Should we have it sent off for analysis?' she asked, eyebrows raised, as she walked into her office, returning unexpectedly early from a meeting.

It was the first time she had seen Josie lost for words.

Refusing a slice of mud cake at Adam's birthday morning tea started off the next round of gossip. As appealing as the rich treat looked Beth had the beginnings of a migraine and chocolate always made it worse.

'I bet it's Weight Watchers,' Josie said to Leanne as they stood at the communal filing basket later that morning. 'You have to pledge to pass up the good stuff most of the time to save your points.'

'Points?'

'Yeah, you know, different foods have different points. Chocolate uses heaps of points but a carrot for example has hardly any. So you have a maximum number of points for the week and you use them how you like.'

'Sounds complicated.'

'It's not that hard, and there's an app. She's always got her phone with her.'

Josie either didn't know or didn't care that her voice carried into the surrounding offices. Despite her amusement, Beth was mildly insulted. Being tall meant she could get away with carrying a few extra kilos and like every woman she did want to lose two or three. But she wasn't quite ready for weigh ins or the points system yet.

Besides, Josie was hardly one to talk. Everybody knew that while she publicly filled in her uniform order form as size 12, she secretly faxed the clothing company later amending it to size 16.

Leanne nodded. 'Could be I guess, but don't you have to be kind of uh, fat, to go there? She has a nice enough figure.'

Josie busied herself putting some reports in sequence to hide her blush. 'I really wouldn't know, I'm just going by what I've heard other people say about it.'

Leanne nodded and let it rest. She didn't have the energy to be harangued yet again about the thin genes she had been blessed with.

* * * * *

As the fourth Saturday of the month approached, Beth began working on her speech. Gordon had jokingly called it her "initiation" to the group and she was determined to get it right. She even started eating lunch at her desk so she could spend more time on it.

Gordon had told her not to stress – that it was not make or break – but she didn't see it like that. Beth had done enough public speaking to be able to gauge audience reaction quickly and she couldn't bear the thought of pouring her heart out only to receive blank stares of disinterest or worse still looks of pity because it was so bad.

Merrily typing away one lunchtime, Beth finally understood the saying "in the zone". It was like nothing around her mattered – the traffic noise outside, the constant hum of the printer just outside her door or the squeal of the fax machine. All she cared about were the words in front of her.

So, it was a rude shock when her computer screen suddenly froze. She paused for a moment, waiting for it to come back to life. Maybe she had just been typing too fast, she thought wryly.

After thirty seconds with no response, she started shaking her mouse. Still nothing. Getting a little more desperate she hit the home key and got the same result.

Noooo!

Beth had deliberately set the document to save only on her memory stick because she didn't want any evidence of it on her work computer. But that was neither here nor there when said document was displayed on her monitor in a 16-point font for all to see.

After five nerve-wracking minutes Beth yanked the memory stick out of the USB drive. There was still no response and her words remained stuck on the screen. Drumming her fingers on the desk she pondered her next move. IT had a strict policy that any computer problems had to be referred to them and under no circumstances were you supposed to reset your own machine.

Peering out her office door Beth could see Josie approaching. Still miffed about the whole gym thing, of late she had been even more nasty than usual. Beth's heart started to pound at the thought of the other woman discovering her secret and blabbing it to the rest of the staff.

Too bad about IT policy she decided, and reached down and hit the power switch. Her screen went blank just as Josie reached her doorway, where she paused to direct a cool stare at Beth, before continuing down the hallway.

Although she feigned innocence, the computer blip that caused the office server to crash was eventually traced back to Beth's computer. All the staff watched as Adam strode down towards her office and closed the door with a resounding click.

Beth met his eyes briefly then looked down again. 'I'm sorry,' she mumbled.

Adam shook his head. 'I'm supposed to be reading you the riot act, you know,' he said in a mock stern voice. 'We could have lost vital client files and other office documents, not to mention the hour of wasted productivity.'

Beth nodded. 'Sorry,' she said again.

'As luck would have it, the backup had just finished so no real harm was done.'

'That's good to hear.'

'I guess that Word document must be something confidential then.'

Startled, Beth looked up again, then nodded slowly.

'I didn't look at it,' he assured her, 'and I binned it before anybody else did.'

'Thanks,' Beth whispered.

'Look I'm not sure what's going on with you, Beth, but people are starting to talk. You've always been well respected around here so whatever it is I just hope it's worth it. You don't want to mess up all your hard work.'

Beth met his gaze for a long moment before replying. 'Yes,' she said, 'to me it's definitely worth it.'

'Well. in that case, consider yourself officially chastised.'

'I'm self-flagellating on the inside.'

They both laughed and Adam stood to leave. He had his hand on the doorknob when he suddenly turned back around. 'So, how about that drink you've been rain-checking me for months?' he murmured, as colour flushed his neck and face. 'I reckon you owe met at least a light beer.'

Beth's eyes met his for a moment. He really was kind of cute in a nerdy way and he'd just saved her skin. Why not?

'Sure. Friday after work?'

Adam couldn't contain his grin. 'Yeah, you bet!'

*B*eth was startled by the sound of applause.

Looking up, she smiled shyly and was greeted with grins of encouragement in return as well as many compliments.

'Great piece,' Gordon said warmly. 'We're so glad you took the leap of faith and joined us here.'

'Fantastic,' agreed Jeannie. 'You've got a real knack with humour.'

'You're a writer all right,' added Larry. 'Don't let them accountants drum it out of you any longer.'

'Thank you!' she said, still a little stunned.

Clutching her sheaf of papers, she sat down and grinned again.

Sure, it was just a small step. After all the Westlands Writers Group was hardly the breeding ground for the Pulitzer Prize. But it was the small step that just might lead her somewhere.

The meeting had been a good reality check too, Beth acknowledged, as she drove home. She knew now that writing was a tough gig and that beyond an absolute miracle she had no hope of earning anywhere near what she did in her current job. She would have to rethink her bold plans to immediately quit Lloyd and Morgan and leave the corporate world behind. But she was willing to make a start and dedicate at least a small part of her energy to the creative side she had locked away for so long.

In just two hours today she had been energised by the ideas and tips that had flowed around her, the most important of which was to *make* time to write.

She wasn't sure yet which she would sacrifice – her lunch hour, gym visits, TV viewing or even sleep – but she was going to find half an hour a day to put pen to paper.

Starting tomorrow.

Because tonight she had her first official date with Adam.

GOOD THINGS

Susanne savoured the silence as she wandered around her photography studio. This was her sacred hour, her "me" time, away from the demands of three young children and running a highly successful business. At this hour she could simply look at the stunning landscape shots displayed around the beautifully lit room and fill her conscious mind with the words on the far wall – *Always do right and good things will come to you.* It had long been her mantra and was the theme that ran through her merchandise – bookmarks, greeting cards, fridge magnets and journals, not to mention her daily gratitude calendar. This in itself was something to be grateful for, because her merchandise was the passive income that allowed her to indulge in several not for profit projects, like the free photography lessons at the community centre and donating high end photographic equipment to low socio-economic schools. Although Susanne had never set out to become known for her philanthropy, as well as her camera skills and positive attitude, the media had been kind to her and she was savvy enough to embrace the positive attention.

Given that she never watched breakfast TV, Susanne knew nothing of the media pack assembling outside the office of her close friend, celebrity agent, Jo deValla. The headline they were chasing was made for the early news - *Empire of Positivity and Good Deeds Built On Stolen Money!* Those not familiar with Susanne's background browsed her blog on their phones as they waited for Jo to emerge. It wasn't a unique story – a woman on the cusp of bankruptcy turning her life around by believing in herself and following her passion. The spin was her claim that "the universe" had delivered her big break because she'd stayed true to her belief of doing "right". But now there were allegations that Susanne had managed to edit out at least one unsavoury deed from her resume – a deed that had allowed her to succeed so spectacularly.

It was only when Susanne switched her phone back on that she got the first hint something was amiss. Dozens of missed calls flashed on her screen as well as numerous text messages. Seconds later there was a loud banging on the door. Alarmed that something might be wrong with one of the children, Susanne opened the door to find Jo, the most glamourous woman she knew, standing there in a tracky dacks and a hoodie, without a skerrick of makeup on. With tears streaming down her face, she bowed her head. 'I'm so sorry, Susie! You were right all along and now I've ruined everything.'

'Right about what?'

'About Jimmy! About the money! He found out and now he's blabbing it to the world.'

Her eyes like saucers, Susanne grabbed her friend by the arm and pulled her inside. 'But how?'

'He's got bank records. I don't know how he accessed your account—' Jo's voice trailed off as she looked at her friend. 'Tell me you opened a new account or at least changed your password.'

Slumping onto the nearest chair Susanne put her head in her hands. 'No, I didn't. I meant to, of course, but—'

Pacing in a tight circle, Jo wrung her hands. 'Oh Susie, we're really in trouble now. The press are outside my office as we speak. It's the headline story on Sunrise.'

There was silence for a moment as both women contemplated their predicament. But, finally, Susanne straightened her back, took a deep breath and looked her friend in the eye. 'If the press is on it, we don't have much time before they come here, do we?'

Wordlessly Jo shook her head.

'Then I guess we'd better get our stories straight.'

rriving at work on a bleak Monday morning, Susanne's heart sank when she realised the door was unlocked. Not because she was worried she'd left it that way, rather because it meant her boss, Alistair, was on the premises. Hidden away on the second floor of a carpet cleaning business, Debts Collect did not advertise its address, and Alistair only showed up sporadically, usually when there was a problem of some kind.

'Susanne, good morning,' he said, appearing from behind the partition near the door. A feeble attempt to keep Susanne safe should some disgruntled debtor discover their address, it was more of a hindrance than anything else.

'Hello Alistair.' Forcing a smile, Susanne made her way to her desk and sat down.

'Susanne, we need to talk. About your financial situation, specifically.'

With great effort, Susanne kept her voice neutral. 'I don't think that's any of your business, Alistair.'

'I'm afraid it is when your name shows up on the latest monthly report.'

Jaw dropping, Susanne clutched a hand to her chest. '*What?*' As horrible as her situation was, she was on top of it, just. Borrowing from Peter to pay Paul had become her speciality and she had made arrangements with every creditor. How could she be on Alistair's report?

Sighing, Alistair sat on the edge of her desk. 'It's a mobile phone bill. Twelve grand. It's been in arrears for a few months, but it really spiked after the SIM card was used in the USA recently, Hawaii, in fact. Hundreds of texts and calls and data by the mile. Now, I know for a fact you haven't been to Hawaii, so I'm assuming it's a SIM you may have purchased for someone else. Any idea who that may be?'

Exhaling sharply, Susanne held out her hand for the

paperwork. 'Thank you, Alistair. I will take care of it. I'm so very sorry about the oversight.'

'You know I run a clean business here, Susanne, but rest assured I know people. I have the means to track somebody down, shake them up a bit. Make them reconsider their position.'

Forcing the fake smile she'd become a master at showing, Susanne shook her head. 'I thank you most sincerely, Alistair, for your kind offer. But it's not your problem. I'll work it out.'

Always do right and good things will come to you.

Her life mantra came to Susanne's mind as she picked up the newest edition of Woman's Day at the checkout that evening. Inhaling deeply, she pinched herself on the arm. It was a technique she had found on an internet forum about dealing with emotional trauma. Apparently, it was a circuit break to prevent lapsing into the same negative response at the sight or memory of painful stimuli. Most of the time it worked, to a degree, at least. But not today. Today the discomfort of the pinch faded in comparison to the jolt of pain she felt at the sight of the cover story. A jolt so deep it felt like a punch to the solar plexus.

"James and his new love holiday in Hawaii", the headline read, accompanied by a photo of a couple embracing near the Duke Kahanamoku statue on Waikiki Beach. Flipping the pages over, Susanne's chest clenched at the montage of snaps, all featuring actor James Mitchell and a blonde waif in a tiny red bikini frolicking in the water and embracing on the sand. The accompanying story told of James' meteoric rise to fame after a low budget telemovie went viral and speculated that he was now being beckoned by Hollywood producers.

Inhaling again, Susanne tried to ignore the new pain in her shoulder. A pain so real it felt like somebody was poking her.

It took her a moment to realise that somebody was actually tapping her on the back, none too gently, either.

'Excuse me!' An irate voice broke into Susanne's foggy brain space. 'Are you going through or not?'

Forcing her eyes away from the magazine, Susanne turned to see a woman in a Commonwealth Bank uniform with a loaded trolley. Arms folded, she was glaring at Susanne.

Nodding, Susanne shoved the magazine back on the rack and dropped her armful of groceries on the checkout conveyor belt. The lean cuisine chicken curry, mini carton of milk and half loaf of bread felt like a neon sign that spelled out her status as a thirty-two-year-old spinster who lived alone in a dingy flat. Unlike the woman behind her, who clearly had a horde of hungry teenagers at home, going by the contents of her trolley.

The Woman's Day wouldn't leave Susanne alone as she made her way home. First the cover appeared in supersize on the billboard outside the newsagent, then the woman sitting next to her on the bus pulled out a copy of the magazine and started reading it. Noticing the way Susanne was staring numbly at the images on the page, the woman put a hand on her chest and sighed. 'Isn't he gorgeous? Shame he's taken. He's from Brisbane, you know. Apparently, he used to live in Toowong.'

Forcing what she hoped was a smile, Susanne nodded. 'I had heard that.' Tearing her eyes away from the offending magazine, she stood and made her way to the front of the bus, ready to disembark two stops early to avoid sending her GO card into arrears.

The landlord was stretching credibility calling it a granny flat. To Susanne's mind it was more of a converted garden shed. So much so that the smell of fertiliser still lingered. However, it was a roof over her head and, more importantly, in her very limited price range, so Susanne didn't dwell too much on the cramped space she now called home. Pulling the screen door open, she groaned as a pile of mail spilled at her feet. It wasn't that Susanne disliked mail per se, it was just that everything delivered to her these days came in a dreaded window envelope and contained the word OVERDUE. Dropping the envelopes on the couch, she decided to eat before facing more bills.

Heating her lean cuisine in the ancient microwave she'd found at a garage sale seemed to take forever. Given its age and low wattage it was lucky the device still worked at all Susanne thought, clearing a space on the couch to sit. When the welcome ping finally sounded, Susanne grabbed the container with a tea towel, stabbed the plastic on the top and collapsed gratefully on the couch to enjoy Home and Away.

The credits had just started to roll when her mobile rang. She didn't need to check the screen to see who it was.

'Hi,' her friend Jo chirped. 'How are Alf and Ailsa and the gang?'

Gathering an ancient crocheted knee rug around her, Susanne made a face, even though Jo couldn't see her response. 'Come on, Jo, it's my one vice. And you know quite well that Ailsa died years and years ago.'

'I'm just teasing. How was your day?'

'Uh, fine.'

'Come on, Sus, you've gotta let it out sometime. Swear at me or scream or something.'

'What's the point? I'd still be in the same situation.'

'I take it you saw the Woman's Day?'

'How could I not?'

Susanne could picture her friend with fists clenched, her fine features twisted into a grimace. 'If I could get my hands on that creep, I swear…'

'Don't waste your energy on it, Jo. He was my mistake, not yours.'

'Yeah, but you only met him because of me. I wish I'd never invited you to that party.'

'I'm okay, Jo. I've always been a worker. I'll just put my head down and tough it out. In a few years I can be debt free again.'

'I could seriously start a Twitter campaign or call A Current Affair. Once it's out there his *new* agent would probably pay us off to keep you quiet.'

'Jo, please don't. I do not want to be that scorned woman pleading pathetically on TV or social media. You know my mantra.'

Taking a deep breath, Jo paused a moment before replying. 'Come on, Sus, I just don't think those words are doing you any favours. You have to stand up for yourself and take revenge when required.'

'I don't need revenge. Everything will be okay.'

'All right, fine. Live like a pauper while he lives like a king. But will you at least come over for dinner tomorrow? I've done a wardrobe clear out too and there's a big bag of stuff you can have.'

Susanne's heart swelled, not only at the kind invitation but at the thought of the money she could save. Skipping lunch tomorrow would leave room for a big dinner and Jo always sent her home with leftovers that would feed her for another day or two. And new clothes, especially the designer ones Jo wore, were a dreamed of luxury these days. 'Thanks, Jo. I'd love to.'

Half an hour later she was on her second glass of very cheap wine and almost to the bottom of the pile of mail. As much as she had reassured Jo she was managing, Susanne's financial status was bleaker than she was willing to admit, even to herself. Of chief concern were the credit card bills, with their exorbitant interest rates. With the interest piling on each month and forcing up the minimum payment, Susanne was the proverbial rat on the maze, running ever harder to meet her commitments. While Alistair had managed to get her a three-month extension on the phone bill, she knew it was only prolonging the agony. The irony that she worked in a debt collection agency was not lost on her as she put her head in her hands and sobbed, pushing the remainder of the pile away to be tackled tomorrow.

Susanne did her best to block out the traffic noise as she walked along the busy road the next morning. Walking to work had just become a necessity. Sure, she'd have to get up half an hour earlier from now on and walk home in the dark in winter, but it would leave more money in her pocket for groceries.

Crossing the road, Susanne headed past the newsagent on the corner, where the Woman's Day cover loomed large yet again. At the café next door, two young women gushed over the pictures of James in Hawaii. What would they say if they knew she had given three years of her life to the charmingly irresponsible Jimmy Jones, as James Mitchell was previously known? Would they admire him as much if they knew that he spent his days attending acting workshops and his nights performing in community theatre productions while Susanne slaved away at the debt collection agency from eight until five and stacked shelves at Coles three nights per week to support him?

'You're such a trouper, Susie,' Jimmy used to tell her when she arrived home at eleven p.m., dead on her feet. 'It'll all be worth it when I crack the big time and you can do that photography course you're always talking about.'

'And have a baby?' she would gently remind him.

'Absolutely, Suse. Not right away, of course, but definitely some time. Now sit down and I'll make you a cup of tea.'

His tea was horrible. Jimmy always used the water from the tap, rather than the filtered jug Susanne kept in the fridge and insisted that heating it in the microwave was easier than boiling the kettle. He never remembered she drank it black, always splashing in far too much of the full cream milk he loved and loading it with sugar. But Susanne had taken the lukewarm mug from him each time, pretending to be grateful, while forcing away the thought that he might have kept some dinner for her.

Always do right and good things will come to you, Susanne used to chant to herself, as she cleaned the flat on Saturday mornings while Jimmy slept in, tired after partying with the cast of his latest play. It was only a matter of time before Jimmy's big break came, everybody said so. Then it would be her turn to pursue her dreams. Susanne had priced the camera she wanted, a Nikon SLR. It was out of reach right now, but one day she'd own it, and she'd have her own photography business too, once she'd done a TAFE course. She'd dreamed of the children she'd have too – two, or maybe even three with her blue eyes and Jimmy's chestnut curls.

Unfortunately, Susanne's belief she was "doing right" hadn't stopped Jimmy from dumping her the week after he was cast in a major film. He hadn't even had the guts to tell her in person, choosing instead to send his new PA over with a list of belongings to collect. Susanne was too stunned to protest as the dewy skinned teenager gathered CDs, the Play Station console and clothes, including the designer leather jacket she was still paying off. Her few timid attempts to contact him afterwards had resulted in a letter from a solicitor with accusations of stalking and threats of a restraining order. It was at that point she'd decided to let it go, even though Jo had urged her to take it further.

'It's my fault,' Susanne said as her friend helped her pack up their flat before eviction proceedings began. 'Everything is in my name. Jimmy liked to keep his financial dealings off the grid. He doesn't like banks.'

'Well it's very convenient to dislike banks yet still avail yourself of their services via someone else's credit rating, isn't it?'

'Yes, I suppose it is.'

* * * * *

Susanne had many moments to doubt her mantra over the following year but finally things began to turn around. Securing her old job at Coles, she once again stacked shelves at night, as well as selling Tupperware, cosmetics and lingerie, via party plans, on the weekend. With Alistair's help she consolidated her debts into one loan with a longer term but smaller repayments. Although she tried not to think about Jimmy, the Woman's Day ensured she was aware of his continuing success. As well as three Hollywood movie roles, Jimmy was now the face of a new men's cologne and had his own sunglasses range. If Susanne had moments where she wondered why the good things she was owed had gone to Jimmy instead of her, she never voiced them, although Jo did.

'Seriously, Sus, can we agree once and for all that your mantra is an unrealistic fantasy?' Jo said as they enjoyed a coffee one Sunday morning.

'No! I'll never stop believing it. Look how far I've come this year. My debt is under control, I'm managing my repayments and finding the housesitting job means I'll be debt free six months sooner.'

'Yeah, in four long years! It's a very weird way to view your dire financial affairs.'

'I'm looking on the bright side. I could have gone bankrupt or suffered a nervous breakdown instead.'

Shaking her head, Jo reached over and grabbed Susanne's hands. 'What if I told you your money problems are solved?'

'What?'

'You heard me. I got an amazing phone call yesterday. Remember that stupid steampunk/horror movie Jimmy was involved in about six years ago? Shipyard Demons?'

'Yeah, I remember. I had to wash his muddy costumes. I don't think he ever got paid and they never released it anyway.'

'Well, they re-edited the movie, added some special effects and sold it to a new offbeat streaming service, that is actually called Offbeat, and it is going gangbusters. There's talk of a series too. Now, given that Jimmy's character died he won't be in the series, obviously, but they have paid him royalties for the movie.'

'Why are you telling me this? So I can get annoyed that he is earning even more money?'

Jo shook her head. 'Of course not! It's for the opposite reason. Even though I'm no longer Jimmy's agent, they are working on the contract he signed for the movie. As you know, he never had a bank account, so they are forwarding the royalties to me as per the arrangement we made back then. I, in turn, will be forwarding them to your bank account.'

Susanne's eyes widened. 'But you can't!'

'I can, actually. Even though he requested that any earnings be paid to him in cash via me, he was required to nominate a bank account as well, as per company policy. He gave me your details.'

'You have to tell him then.'

'I tried to contact Jimmy many times and, like you, was threatened with a solicitors letter. I'm not planning on trying again.'

'But won't the film company tell Jimmy?'

'No, like I said, they are the instructions on the contract he signed. As far as the production company are concerned, they are paying him via me. They didn't even make provision for royalties, it was all about getting exposure and a small fee if the movie got a cinema release.'

'So why *are* they paying him, then?'

'They're just being careful to dot their i's and cross their t's now they've sold the movie on.'

'What if he finds out?'

'He won't. It's an Australian streaming service watched by alternative types and he's way too mainstream these days for it to even be on his radar. Not to mention he was still calling himself Jimmy Jones then, so they won't link it on the internet. All contact regarding the money is through me as per the iron clad contract he signed. No doubt it was to stop any gangsters he owed money to going after his earnings.'

'You're really going to put the money in my account?'

Jo nodded.

'How much are we talking about?'

'Fifty grand.'

Clutching her chest, Susanne stared at her friend. Then she fainted.

Although Susanne insisted she was all right, the paramedics highly recommended she be transported to hospital. Six hours later she was settled into a bed with her right arm in a cast. A chart for half hourly neurological observations hung on the end of the bed. A head injury was still a possibility and she would need to be observed overnight.

It was only when the nurse left that Jo was finally allowed in to see her. Setting her takeaway coffee cup on the bedside locker she leaned in to hug her friend, careful not to knock her plastered arm. 'Susanne Wright, you will be the death of me!' she scolded. 'You hit the ground like a rock, I thought you'd fractured your skull for sure.'

'Wasn't I just telling you how lucky I was?'

Pulling the visitors chair over, Jo sat down. 'Yeah, before my big news rendered you unconscious.'

'News?' said Susanne, furrowing her brow.

'You don't remember? Oh no, you have got a head injury! How many fingers am I holding up?' Jo thrust a clenched fist in front of Susanne's face.

Susanne laughed. 'I'm sorry, I was just kidding. Of course I remember your news! I was delirious with joy until I realised I can't keep the money.'

'What do you mean you can't keep it? What could possibly be the problem with a genuine windfall presented to you at the moment of your greatest need?'

'The money isn't mine.'

'Technically true, but all the debt Jimmy racked up wasn't yours either. Sounds like a fair swap to me.'

Susanne had to concede Jo's line of thought made sense.

'Jimmy is making two million a movie, not to mention the sunglasses and that stink water he's peddling. Fifty grand is like a week's wages. He owes you, Susie. Take the money!'

Susanne buried her head in her hands for a moment before looking her best friend in the eye. 'Do you really think I should?'

'Absolutely.'

* * * * * *

Jo knew that money didn't buy happiness, but she was of the opinion that it definitely helped. After she'd bequeathed Susanne Jimmy's earnings, the change in her friend was nothing short of amazing. Once Susanne paid her debts off, her life transformed around her just the way she'd always dreamed, and Jo loved witnessing each new blessing that came her way. First was the photography course and the camera she'd coveted for so long, and then she met Nate, who was as honest and straightforward as Jimmy had been the opposite. Jo had been there at her first exhibit, had helped plan her studio launch, was bridesmaid at her wedding and among the first to hold her children after they were born. If she was completely honest, there were moments when Jo envied Susanne as she quietly made her mark on the world without all the stress and drama her own job entailed.

When Susanne insisted that her life mantra be included in all facets of her photography business, Jo was a little surprised at the uncharacteristic duplicity but didn't see the harm in it. Nobody needed to know that Susanne's change of fortune had come about by doing the opposite of what she preached, and Jo would never tell. People loved all that positive affirmation stuff and it was a great little earner for Susie, allowing her to work less while her children were small. Susanne still genuinely believed it, though, and Jo had given up trying to convince her otherwise. Maybe she'd just worked too many years with people who were only in it for themselves to believe that anybody cared about doing right anymore.

Although they never really talked about Jimmy, especially once Nate came into Susanne's life, Jo still followed his career. She heard about the Porsche he drove, the lavish parties he threw, the holidays on luxury yachts and the never-ending stream of women who frequented his Hollywood Hills mansion. Because of her job, though, Jo was also privy to the less endearing gossip that was starting to filter through the grapevine, stories about huge gambling debts and unpaid bills all around Tinseltown. Given that he had treated Susanne like his own personal bank, this was not surprising to Jo and she wondered, yet again, what her kind and generous friend had ever seen in such a morally, not to mention financially, corrupt person.

While the early reports were dismissed as rumours, Jimmy's part in an embezzlement scam sealed his fate as a Hollywood has been, just as fast as he'd risen to stardom. Fired from his latest movie and evicted from his home due to rent arrears, Jimmy disappeared from the limelight and was last seen boarding a flight to the Cayman Islands, where he had reportedly stashed some emergency funds. Jo was just happy that Susanne no longer watched the news, believing it to attract negative energy into her home.

* * * * *

It was true that Jimmy eventually landed in the Cayman Islands, but his stay there was much shorter than anticipated. 'Sorry, Jim, I can't be seen hanging out with you,' his fellow Aussie actor, Max McCreagh, said when Jimmy turned up on his holiday rental doorstep. '*I'm* the new big thing in Hollywood now and I need to protect my image.'

'What about the pact we made when we arrived in LA together? Brothers for life and all that.'

'It's a fickle world, mate. You might just have to go home and hide out there for a while.'

'I don't have enough for a plane ticket. I had to sell my iPad to make it here.'

'Well, like I said, you can't stay. You can have the couch tonight and I'll spot your fare home but that's it.'

It was an incognito James Martin who slunk into a back-row seat on budget airline Fly4Less, flying economy for the first time in many years. Exhausted after routing via Miami and Atlanta on night flights, Jimmy slumped against the window as the plane rose over Los Angeles and slept almost all the way to Brisbane. It was only when they hit a patch of turbulence during the descent that he finally woke up. Rubbing his bleary eyes, he did his best to avoid interacting with the passenger sitting next to him, but the young man had other ideas. Staring openly, he gasped in excitement. 'It is you! When you first got on I thought you must just be a lookalike, but when your hat fell off I was pretty sure! You're the guy from—'

Sighing, Jimmy gave a fake smile. 'West Coast Hero?'

'No.'

'Red Handed? The Last Big Thing? Who's That Guy?'

'Come off it, I don't watch any of that Hollywood junk. You're the guy from Shipyard Demons! Adreas, right?'

Scratching his head, Jimmy frowned at his seat mate. 'How have you seen that? *I've* never even seen it.'

'It was on Offbeat. I've watched it heaps of times. I even joined the online fan group.'

'What the hell is Offbeat?'

'It's one of those internet streaming channels, it's got all the good stuff.'

'I've been living in America, I never knew they released it.'

'It was ages ago. There's a spin off series too. Obviously Andreas wasn't in that, seeing that you died and all, but it was a big hit.'

'Why didn't they tell me about it?'

'I don't know, mate, but you must have been pocketed a nice pay cheque.'

'No, I didn't. Not one cent and I could certainly use some cash.'

'You'd better get onto your agent then, pronto.'

'Oh, yes, I will. Don't you worry about that,' Jimmy said, a smile spreading across his face as Brisbane airport came into view.

*I*t was a composed, immaculately groomed Jo who eventually fronted the media, after calling an official press conference outside her office. She'd always believed herself to be the practical one in their friendship, but after the events of the last hour she'd seen a new side to Susanne. While she'd expected her friend to crumble under the stress of it all, Jo had been the one who'd needed to be calmed and prepared for the onslaught while Susanne called the shots.

'Good morning, all. As you are aware, my former client, James Mitchell, aka Jimmy Jones, is accusing myself and my close friend, Susanne Wright, of stealing money from him. While it is true that royalties from the movie Shipyard Demons were forwarded to me in trust for James, it is not true that said funds were used by Susanne Mitchell to develop her business.'

'But James has got bank records that show that sum being transferred from you to Ms Wright!' said a young woman in the front row.

'Yes, that's correct. To her bank account as per contract instructions.'

'Why didn't he have his own bank account?'

'I don't know.'

'But you still forwarded it to Susanne even when you knew they weren't together anymore.'

'Yes, I did know that, but a contract is a contract. I was following instructions.'

'Why didn't you tell him about it?' asked a pudgy middle-aged man on the outskirts of the group.

'All attempts by myself and Susanne to contact James have been rejected. I can show you a solicitor's letter if you like, with threats of stalking charges.'

'Why would he do that?'

'I suspect Mr Mitchell was trying to avoid me because he had a guilty conscience about jumping ship to a new agent without paying my finder's fee. I was the one who secured him his breakout role and orchestrated his name and image change, after all. As for Ms Wright, you'd have to ask him that.'

'In that case where is James' cash then? The bank records show it being transferred out two days later.'

'Susanne simply moved it into a different account.'

'Why didn't you send his new agent a cheque?'

Jo shrugged. 'Perhaps I could have, but it wasn't my job to chase him up. Mr Mitchell knew where I was and, like I said, he had previously shunned all attempts at contact.'

'So, you're saying you'll pay him then? With interest?' called the sharp faced woman on the low rent current affairs show.

'Yes, of course. If Mr Mitchell had simply contacted me in the first place instead of going to the media this could have been avoided altogether.'

Although they did their best to keep the scandal alive, the media scrum knew their headline story was a washout and after a few more questions were batted right back at them by Jo's careful, measured answers they began to leave, phones to their ears, seeking out their next assignments. It was only after the last one departed that Jo went back inside the city office block and took the lift to her office, where Susanne waited, gazing serenely out the window.

Staring at her friend in wonder, Jo held both hands up, palms out. 'They bought it, just like you said. I'm stunned, quite frankly.'

'Jimmy claimed we stole his money, we had a plausible answer and offered to give it back with interest. There's no headline in that.'

'True. But I'm also stunned that the most honest person I know could suggest I lie so openly.'

'You didn't lie.'

'Come on, Sus! We both know where you got the money to start your business. It's just lucky you now have the means to give it back so quickly. I love you dearly, you know that, but you can't pretend there wasn't deception in what we did. It was my idea, I completely admit, but you went along with it. Your little mantra wasn't anywhere in all this.'

'Oh, but it was, Jo. It was everywhere in all this.'

'How, exactly?'

'I didn't use Jimmy's money. Not one cent of it. It's been sitting in the bank since the day you transferred it to me.'

Jo's mouth dropped open. 'Seriously?'

'Uh huh.'

'Then how did you pay your debts and buy your camera?'

'I almost used it. I was at the bank and ready to pay out the loan when I decided I couldn't go through with it. I opened a Bonus Saver account instead and that's when the magic started happening.'

'Magic?'

'I was psyching myself up to call Alistair and ask for my job back when I got an email from Global Trek, you know the hiking adventure company? I'd submitted a photo of King's Canyon I took years ago with my old 35 mil film camera and they wanted to use it on a billboard. Thirty grand, just like that. A few weeks later an insurance policy my grandparents set up for me matured. Another ten grand. Then, my amazing friend got my name out there for my first photographic exhibition and before I knew it I was in business. I think you know the rest.'

Jo's mouth was still open. 'I think we need to trademark

your mantra.'

'Already done, my dear friend. I may be ridiculously optimistic but I'm not silly.'

'No, you are most certainly not.'

PSEUDO

$\mathcal{T}$ hanks to the timer on her De'Longhi, Isabelle woke each morning to the smell of freshly brewed coffee. Stretching leisurely, she inhaled the decadent aroma and snuggled under the covers for a few minutes longer, safe in the knowledge her first lecture for the day wasn't until ten o'clock.

Ah, the luxury of student life!

As always, Isabelle began her day by looking up at her image hanging on the wall at the opposite end of her bed. Her purchase, and subsequent framing, of an official print of her first and only front-page article hung there as a constant reminder of just what she had managed to pull off.

Even though she'd known it was coming, seeing her image splashed across the front page of *The Courier Mail* had still taken Isabelle by surprise. Not only was it a much bigger picture than she had expected but she had also made the Saturday edition, with its much larger circulation!

Isabelle could imagine her old school teachers and former classmates picking up the paper and their eyes widening in amazement as they read the headline 'The Face of UQ'. They must certainly have wondered how Isabelle Mathers, a below average student with an OP in the twenties teamed with zero ambition, had managed such a feat.

According to the article it was by way of hard work and soul searching. Isabelle had described herself as a 'late bloomer' who took some time out to explore the working world and 'took the alternative scenic route' to bolster her school results to gain entry to the institution of her choice.

In reality, it had been much easier than that and Isabelle still couldn't quite fathom she had gotten away with it.

$\mathcal{T}$he tiny township of Blue Moon Lake was dark and silent as Isabelle drove along the dirt road to her grandparent's holiday shack. It was looking tired now – being almost 50 years old – but to Isabelle it would always be a magic place, filled with memories of idyllic childhood summer holidays. Grandpa was dead now and Gran had recently moved into a retirement village, but she refused to let the old place be sold – for which Isabelle was very grateful.

During this, her twenty-first year, Isabelle found herself visiting the shack on a depressingly regular basis. Not that it was an awful place to go, rather it was depressing because she had so little else to do with her time. Using reasoning she had borrowed from an episode of *Seinfeld*, Isabelle theorised that if she went to the lake at least she was out of her flat. So while she may do as little at the shack as she would at home, she was 'away for the weekend' and thus not *as much* of a loser.

The trip to Blue Moon Lake took two hours and twenty minutes door to door, so if she left Brisbane by seven Isabelle was at the house by nine thirty, just in time to open a bottle of wine and watch a DVD on her laptop. Gran and Grandpa had always had an iron clad rule there was to be no TV in the house and Isabelle couldn't bring herself to break it.

By the time Saturday afternoon rolled around, Isabelle had worked her way through two seasons of *Seinfeld* and all her food rations. Quiet even in the summer months, Blue Moon Lake was like a tomb in winter, especially on bleak, rainy days like today.

Shifting her position on the sagging armchair, she unwrapped the last Mintie from the bag and popped it in her mouth, pondering just how she'd ended up here, pathetic and lonely.

Having no interest in school, she had attended for social

rather than academic reasons. Her boyfriend, Nick, and best friend, Gina, were of the same mindset and all three had exited the school gates with little more than signed uniforms and a class photo.

They hadn't let it hold them back though. Leaving their small home town and sharing a flat in Brisbane had been a blast. They soon realised there were entry-level jobs out there that didn't require great school results or even good results.

Totally wrapped up in their own little world, the trio rarely socialised with their workmates or old school friends who had also made the move to Brissie. Instead they were content to spend their evenings and weekends ensconced on the couch watching movies, spending time on-line and playing video games. Eating out meant a trip to Maccas or KFC, so there was no need to worry about how little they earnt.

Sure, they moaned about their horrible jobs, but it was just what people did. They didn't care enough to do anything about it.

Caught up in her reverie, Isabelle jumped when her mobile phone rang. Checking the screen before she connected, she rolled her eyes and shook her head. Her boss Edward – perfect! She could just ignore the call, but past experience told her he would just keep ringing at increasingly frequent intervals until she answered.

'Hello.'

'Yes, Isabelle, I really need to speak to you. Can you come into the office in one hour?'

'No, I'm away for the weekend, Edward. Is there a problem?'

'No, not one problem specifically – more like a range of them. Come and see me immediately when you arrive on Monday.'

'Yes, Edward,' Isabelle murmured, before disconnecting the call. Tentacles of panic blossomed in her gut, reaching up to encircle her chest and throat. As much as she hated her office job in the small bathroom supply business, she needed it.

Isabelle had been the last man standing when Nick and then Gina decided to get more serious about life. She had ignored the TAFE brochures and laughed when they started applying for better jobs and encouraged her to do the same. She had also ignored the signs that Nick and Gina had become a couple, right until the day they announced they were moving out, together.

'You're never going to amount to anything, Isabelle,' Nick had told her as he hauled boxes of his belongings out the front door.

After she'd gotten over the devastation of being betrayed by the two people closest to her, Isabelle realised what a flow on effect this created. Her social life as she knew it had evaporated in an instant and she was suddenly very much alone, with a horrible job and a massive weekly rent bill.

Thus began her pilgrimages to Blue Moon Lake.

It was getting dark by the time Isabelle trudged down to the general store/newsagent for more supplies. The cosy temperature inside the shop was enticing and, having plenty of time to kill, she took her time flipping through the magazine display and dawdling over her meal selection. Should she get nacho cheese or salsa flavoured corn chips? Caramel chocolate or peppermint? Cookies 'n' cream ice cream or a Vienetta?

Elsie, the elderly shopkeeper, eyed Isabelle suspiciously. They had always had a somewhat hostile association, although Isabelle couldn't put her finger on why. No unpleasant words had ever been exchanged, yet it was clear to both of them that they didn't like each other. Realising it was almost closing time, Isabelle finally made her way to the cash register and dumped her magazines and junk food on the counter.

Elsie rang up the purchases briskly, as if she had far more important things to be doing than serving the likes of a young woman in tracky dacks and thongs. Isabelle had always thought Elsie harboured a secret fantasy that somebody important was going to walk through the shop door one day and she didn't want to be seen associating with the riff raff.

'Anything else then?' Elsie asked, with a tight smile.

Isabelle flashed an insincere grin in return. 'Uh, yes, actually. I'll have a two dollar scratchie thanks. One of those new Rainbow ones.'

Elsie eyed the younger woman for a second, apparently fighting the desire to refuse service. 'You're sure you wouldn't prefer one of these Easter Egg ones?' she asked, indicating the rolls of tickets under the counter. 'They're still perfectly valid even though Easter has been and gone.'

'No, I'd really like a rainbow one, thanks,' Isabelle replied, with another insincere smile. The rainbow tickets were a new promotion with higher jackpots and Elsie had shoved them over to the side, obviously to discourage people buying them until the older stock had gone.

'Right,' Elsie snapped. Leaning over she ripped a ticket off with much more force than necessary and shoved it into the too-small bag she had crammed the rest of Isabelle's purchases in. 'That'll be twenty-three dollars, forty-three thanks.'

Isabelle fought the urge to roll her eyes. Almost two decades after the demise of copper coins, Elsie still insisted on pricing in one and two cent increments and only rounded up, never down. Pulling a fifty dollar note out of her purse, she slapped it down on the counter.

Elsie slapped the change down in much the same way and Isabelle departed without either of them uttering another word.

It wasn't until several hours, and a bottle of wine, later that Isabelle remembered the scratchie. Rummaging through the discarded food wrappings and magazines, she finally came across the ticket. Using her thumbnail, and destroying an expensive acrylic nail in the process, she scratched the silver coating away to reveal three little sailboats. Cool, she thought, I've probably won two bucks and I'll have to go and annoy Elsie a little more by cashing it in tomorrow.

After scratching the prize panel, Isabelle's heart lurched. She must be drunker than she thought! According to the legend, three boats equalled a prize of one hundred and fifty thousand dollars.

Rubbing her eyes and pinching herself to make sure she wasn't dreaming, Isabelle checked the ticket again. Yes, it was definitely right.

She had just become a wealthy young woman!

Not sure of what else to do Isabelle collapsed onto the floor and began to laugh hysterically.

* * * * * *

It took a few weeks for the idea to fully form. Although Isabelle immediately resigned from her job – just before being sacked she suspected – and went to the Golden Casket office in Woolloongabba in person to pick up her prize cheque, she put off telling anybody about her win. She needed time to think and plan…

Naturally enough her first thoughts were of the exotic

travel she could do, the new car and wardrobe…and maybe even a deposit on a unit of her own. But amidst all these materialistic thoughts, Nick's words about her never amounting to anything kept replaying in her head.

Sure, the money would let her do anything she wanted for now, but she would still be unqualified, unemployed *and* lonely. Holidays were not much fun by yourself and who could she invite over to her new place?

The old saying was right, money by itself did not make you happy. No, it would have to be what she did with the money. But what?

The question nagged at Isabelle. Logging onto Facebook one morning she sighed morosely. She hadn't bothered unfriending either Nick or Gina and both their pages were full of fun pictures with their new mates. A few of the girls from school had pages that were similar. countless images of parties and campus life clogged their timelines.

The realisation came to Isabelle gradually. She had thought her friends from school were mad to sign up for years more study when they could be earning money and doing what they liked on the weekends. But she had missed the bigger picture, she hadn't considered the fun factor of student life. It was only now after being stuck in the most un-fun workplace imaginable that she finally got it.

TAFE was an option but the idea didn't overly appeal, mainly because it would seem like she was copying Nick and Gina. Nick's comments still stung and she didn't want to appear to be following his advice.

No, it had to be something bigger and better – like university.

Amid all the daydreams about hanging out on campus and partying on the weekends Isabelle had to keep reminding herself of two key problems; firstly, her abysmal school results and, secondly, the reality she would have to actually study even if she did get in. She had literally never studied in her life.

She was having a pedicure one day when the idea came to her. Why couldn't she just *unofficially* go to uni? It wasn't like school where you had to go to homeroom and have the roll marked after all. Who would actually know she wasn't an enrolled student? Her winnings would provide an income while she embraced the student lifestyle (and all its advantages) without the work.

She had ignored the signs when Nick and Gina had their epiphany but the universe had given her a second chance, she decided gleefully. And unlike them she would barely have to lift a finger!

Buoyed by her brainwave, Isabelle cut short her pedicure, so she could start researching the lifestyle of a pseudo student.

* * * * *

Isabelle was amazed at how her family took the news at face value. Nobody asked to see her acceptance papers, even though she had created a genuine looking set on her computer. Nobody questioned why any self-respecting university would admit her with such poor school results, believing Isabelle's story that life experience was taken into consideration.

When it came to choosing which university to attend, Isabelle knew it would have to be the University of Queensland. With its prestigious reputation, large enrolment (to allow her to blend in), huge range of courses and the fact it was a beautiful campus to boot, it ticked all the boxes.

As the academic year drew closer, Isabelle attended open days and free lectures to familiarise herself with the university scene. Inventing a scholarship to explain her ability to support herself, Isabelle found herself a unit to rent in Toowong, much nicer than the average student could afford.

Shopping for her new life proved to be a lot of fun. A desk and a laptop were necessities, as was a cool backpack. Isabelle adjusted her wardrobe to trendy yet scruffy. This proved to be more expensive than she had imagined, but in the end, she looked the part and that was all that mattered.

The most difficult thing was gaining a student card. Fortunately she had thought ahead and found herself a decent forger on the internet. Isabelle was amazed – and quite disturbed – at the array of false IDs readily available. But, as she kept reminding herself, she wasn't hurting anybody by her actions. She had no intention of pretending to be a doctor, for example, just a nice, general arts student. Obviously her card was useless for anything official, but it would suffice for her needs.

Although very nervous on the first day of O-week, Isabelle soon realised that everybody assumed she was entitled to be there. Nobody asked for her enrolment papers as she attended talks and workshops.

'Gosh this is all so exciting isn't it?' a frizzy haired teenager seated beside Isabelle exclaimed as they awaited an official "welcome to campus" speech.

'Yeah, it is,' she agreed.

'I must admit I'm a bit scared though. I mean, I'm from a tiny town nobody has heard of and I'm living with my great auntie way over in Chermside. What if I don't make any friends?'

'Don't think like that, surely amidst these thousands of people you'll connect with somebody. Hey, you just did. I'm

Isabelle and I'm looking for some new friends too. And I live really close.'

'Saskia,' the young woman replied. 'I'm SO pleased to meet you.'

'Likewise. Now let's listen to this speech, then get out there and become uni students.'

Taking the smorgasbord approach, Isabelle attended about twenty lectures in the first week before honing in on the four subjects she liked most. Unfettered by pre-requisites or other such details, she only chose subjects that interested her and those with a large enrolment so she could remain anonymous.

Despite the fact Isabelle was a few years older than Saskia and worldlier, the pair soon formed a close, genuine friendship. Although she cultivated several casual friendships in her own subjects, Isabelle was glad that Saskia was studying Business. This allowed her to hone in on Saskia's new friends and make them hers too without being closely scrutinised about her studies. She joined some clubs as well to cast her friendship net as far as possible.

As she had anticipated, living so close to campus helped cement Isabelle's unit as a social hub. Far from being annoyed when friends dropped in to hang out or needed a place to crash after a night out, Isabelle loved it. Having no actual uni work to complete, Isabelle's evenings and weekends were free for as much partying as she liked. And party she did, determined to make up for lost time.

* * * * *

The semester moved along much faster than Isabelle had anticipated. Thirteen weeks sounded so distant at the beginning, but now it was almost at an end. Isabelle observed the shift from the cruisy first weeks to the more frantic pace of assessment deadlines. Lecturers became less forgiving and their expectations of their students increased. People started looking serious and determined, the study carrels in the library became a hot destination and stress hung in the air, an almost tangible weight upon the shoulders of every student.

Every student except for Isabelle, as she experienced none of this stress, although her unit showed evidence of it. Piles of textbooks and papers were scattered across her desk, along with photocopies of journal articles. A semester planner was affixed to her wall with assessment dates duly entered.

It was the last week of semester when the journalist approached Isabelle as she walked along Fred Schonell Drive. Feeling at a bit of a loose end because nobody had time to pop around and hang out, she had headed out to uni hoping to bump into somebody and maybe grab a coffee.

'Excuse me, miss, are you a student here?' the young woman asked.

'Uh, yes, I am,' Isabelle replied. Even after a semester, she still hesitated when directly asked that question. Fortunately, it didn't happen very often because as long as you were on campus people just assumed you had the right to be there.

'Great!' the young woman enthused. 'My name is Alison and I'm a journalist at *The Courier Mail*. I'm writing a feature article for education week and I'd love to interview you if you've got time.'

'Um, sure. But why me? I'm sure there's heaps of other more talented students with a more interesting back story than me.'

'No, it's not about that. I'm a real believer in seizing the moment and I've just got a great feeling about you.'

Stretched for time due to another assignment taking much

longer than planned, in reality Alison had a looming deadline and had headed out to UQ on a whim. Forgetting her earlier ideas about seeking out an "against all odds" subject for her article, she had decided to go traditional and couldn't believe her luck when she'd literally almost bumped into somebody who totally fit the bill.

Isabelle hesitated for a second and then nodded. 'Sure, I'd love to.'

'Excellent! Thanks so much,' Alison replied. 'Let's head up to the coffee shop and have a chat.'

* * * * *

Having had no need to flee to Blue Moon Lake for months, it felt a little strange as Isabelle headed down the familiar dirt road. It was ironic too, this time she needed to hide from her friends not hide the fact she had no friends.

Having told her uni pals she was sitting her exams early so as to attend an overseas wedding, Isabelle had to get out of Brisbane for a while and so her old haunt was the obvious choice. It was a shame she wasn't there to bask in the glory of the newspaper article but it couldn't be helped.

Rising early, Isabelle drove into town still in her PJs and collected a paper from the stack outside the general store. Dropping her payment into the honesty box, she realised she should have waited for Elsie to open up so she could gauge her reaction when she realised her brush with fame had finally arrived.

Isabelle had just made herself a coffee when her mobile rang. Reaching over to hit the speaker button she said, 'Hi Mum', without preamble.

'Issie, how did you know it was me?' her mother replied.

'Who else would ring me at six am on a Saturday?' Isabelle didn't bother trying to explain caller ID yet again.

'Ah, I hope I didn't wake you.'

'No, I was up.'

'I thought as much seeing today was the big day. Gosh, Issie, Dad and I are so proud of you! Our daughter chosen as the face of the biggest university in Queensland! It's just incredible. All my friends will be green with envy.'

'It's not that big a deal, really. I just happened to be in the right place at the right time.'

'Well, yes, but I don't just mean the picture. I mean how you got yourself there in the first place. Let's face it, love, you weren't much chop at school and your dad and I did worry about your future. Then out of the blue you pull yourself up by the bootstraps and enrol at university! My secret hope for you was a secretarial course or a hairdressing apprenticeship. Gosh, I get all teary just thinking about it.'

'Come on, Mum, it's not that special. Lots of people go to uni.'

'Not in our family they don't. You're a real pioneer, Issie.'

Isabelle couldn't help but smile at that comment. She was a bit of a pioneer, wasn't she? And the way she figured it, if she expanded her social circle a bit further to include some law or medical students she might just meet someone special and there was her future taken care of.

So much for Nick's dire prediction about her not amounting to anything.

Ah, yes, she was really on her way now.

*F*ortified by a large coffee from her beloved De'Longhi, Isabelle gathered her things together and bundled up in her parka before heading out the door. Winter was definitely biting now and she was really looking forward to the arrival of spring.

Locking her door behind her she checked her watch and realised she would have to walk briskly. Despite living so close to campus she still managed to run late most mornings. Not that it really mattered, but it was something she needed to work on. Then again, the icy snow was still thick on the ground, so it was just as well she had to walk fast.

Learning to dress in layers and discovering the necessity of a beanie, gloves and a scarf were just a few new life experiences Isabelle was coming to terms with. She walked in the middle of the road because it was the driest part and, also, simply because she could. Cars were not common in these parts and their approach could be heard far away in the crisp, unpolluted air.

Half an hour later Isabelle sat in a classroom, where she was, in fact, an officially enrolled student with an authentic student ID card. Yes, it was a remote, regional campus of the University of Western Tasmania with an enrolment of 75, housed in an old high school. Isabelle was enrolled in an Ecology degree, a subject in which, admittedly, she had zero interest. The university campus had no proper library and students had to email requests to the main campus with an average waiting time of five days. And, yes, it did snow there regularly, and the buildings were not centrally heated.

Isabelle had soon learned how the description of a 'cosy' atmosphere, small class sizes and a World Heritage location teeming with wildlife had lured her fellow nature-loving students there, whereas she was there with the sole intention of getting a foot in the door.

It had taken some doing.

While her friends at UQ enjoyed their mid-year holidays Isabelle phoned the admissions office of possibly every tertiary institution in Australia that offered a mid-year intake and was prepared to overlook her tragic OP score. Unsurprisingly, most had passed on the opportunity to welcome her into their student body, but finally good old Western Tassie had come to the rescue. They were nearly as desperate as she was, given that their funding would cease if they couldn't fill their enrolments. Isabelle wasn't sure who was more excited when her application was accepted, them or her.

She didn't plan to stay long term; two semesters should be enough to boost her academic record to an acceptable level. Her aim was to go back to UQ as a real student and earn a degree the normal way.

But UWT had some definite advantages. The cost of living was really cheap and the small class sizes meant that Isabelle got all the help she needed to improve her academic standing. Her nest egg was well invested and she even had a job in the aptly named End of the World Cafe. Things had actually turned out better than she could have imagined.

Reading the paper that night, she came across the story of a woman in Melbourne who had faked not only her enrolment in a law degree, but had also earnt herself a job on the strength of her bogus qualifications. Fortunately her ruse had fallen apart quite spectacularly when she took on her first court case. It had soon become apparent that her knowledge of a courtroom had been gleaned from reading legal thrillers and the judge was forced to declare a mistrial. And now she was looking down the barrel of a jail term for fraud. Not to mention a vicious social media hate campaign from her disgruntled client.

Wow, at least I wasn't that bad, thought Isabelle self-righteously.

Looking up at her newspaper article again Isabelle shuddered. Yes, it did showcase what she had gotten away with but it was also a reminder of her own dishonesty and a warning to never sink that low again.

Isabelle liked to think that she would have eventually decided to abandon her charade, that the reality of being unable to attend a graduation ceremony and the expectation she might be qualified to do something other than entry level jobs might have hit home.

In truth, though, it was the article that had forced her hand. The message from the UQ admissions office had come via *The Courier Mail*. Wanting to profile Isabelle on the university website they had been unable to locate her on their records and were very keen to speak to her. They were assuming it was a spelling error or that she may have enrolled under a different name, but it had been enough to give Isabelle the fright of her life.

Hastily changing her home and mobile phone numbers had given her some breathing space but the thought that people were trying to track her down and that she might be exposed had scared her enough to take a good look at the person she had become.

Yes, Isabelle decided as she set the coffee machine before heading off to bed, she was ashamed of what she had done but she was not totally sorry it had happened. Her experience as a pseudo student had helped her realise that life goals *were* worth working towards in an honest fashion and also that she did want to make something of her life.

By some stroke of luck she had escaped from the whole situation unscathed *and* she had the opportunity to make things right.

Surely that wasn't such a bad thing?

DIAMOND PUDDING

*Q*lbert Smythe deplored nepotism.

Admittedly it was because he came from a family of such low social standing that no nepotistic opportunities were even a remote possibility. Still, that was beside the point. Surely in the twenty-first century jobs should be awarded by merit, not family connections.

He had always believed his boss to be a fair-minded person. Inexperienced at business, but fair. True, he had finagled his way into her company for his own purposes, but that was water under the bridge. His experience and knowledge had made him a shoo in for CEO. Not only had Albert expected the promotion, he had counted on it. While he would never have considered the job ten years ago, his career had fallen on decidedly hard times and he was pragmatic enough to accept that you have to move with the times to stay employed in the food industry when you're on the wrong side of fifty.

For a whole year he had waited. He had turned up to work every day, smiled at the inane questions and put out fires when required. He had constantly reassured his boss that her lack of formal qualifications didn't matter, that in this age of reality TV and social media anybody with a dream could succeed. Most tellingly, though, he'd listened to her complain how lazy and entitled her children could be, which had led Albert to believe she was on the same page as him regarding nepotism.

As Albert expected, the business took off, exceeding all expectations. The voice of reason, he had subtly dropped hints that it was time to take things to the next level and appoint some proper management staff. His boss had been reluctant at first but eventually came to realise that Albert was right. He had prepared himself for the official discussion, had even practised a shocked but happy expression when she announced that the top job was his.

He certainly didn't have to pretend to be shocked when she announced that her daughters were joining the company as Finance and Marketing Managers, respectively, negating the need for a CEO. It had taken every ounce of self-control to not bang his fist on the desk and shout "no fair!" It wasn't like Albert lost out, he got a raise and a bigger office, but he was still a lowly Management Adviser, not a CEO.

That day was a turning point for Albert. He still played the part of the loyal employee, but inwardly he seethed and began planning his revenge.

It wasn't that difficult. He still had contacts in the industry willing to help him in his quest. It had taken weeks of trawling through paperwork but eventually they found the ammunition Albert needed. And, just yesterday, he had taken possession of a document that he was going to present at today's executive staff meeting.

Setting up the large oval table in the board room, he carefully positioned a tall jug of iced water in the centre and square crystal tumblers at the four places at one end. Blank paper and pens were positioned equally carefully. A vase of fresh flowers rounded things out. Then, finally, Albert placed an A4 enveloped containing the explosive document at the head of the table.

The document that would blow this little family affair apart.

*I*t wasn't an easy dessert to make. The diamond pudding consisted of five distinct layers, each needing to be prepared separately and mixed by hand before going in the oven for the precise time. It then needed to be cooled at room temperature for at least three hours before being carefully sliced. If it wasn't for the compliments she received and the fact she loved the pudding so much herself, Libby would never bother making it. A labour of love, her grandmother used to call it, a sentiment Libby agreed with. At the end of the day food was all about love, she supposed, as she carefully hand whipped the egg whites with a whisk. On a whim, she'd decided to enter a cooking competition she'd heard advertised on the radio. Celebrating the old-fashioned cooking movement, the Delightful Dessert Company were seeking out a new signature dessert that would become part of their product range. With a large cash prize and the offer of a job in the company kitchen, Libby was immediately inspired to enter.

Nursing may have been her day job, but Libby had always loved baking and had often fantasised about opening her own café one day. The idea of cooking for a living seemed like paradise compared to night shifts and dealing with the rough and tumble of the mixed medical ward. It had remained a fantasy, however, as bringing up two children alone required a job with a steady pay packet and the bonus of shift allowances and weekend penalty rates.

An hour later, Libby carefully placed the pudding mixture in the fridge and clicked off the video function on her phone. After chilling for three hours the pudding would go in the oven for precisely two and a quarter hours at exactly one hundred and forty-five degrees. The pudding had been perfected over three generations, but the family tradition would almost certainly end with her, Libby thought glumly as she ran hot water into the sink. Neither of her daughters, Cleo and Brianna, showed the slightest interest in cooking. They were both at uni, pursuing important careers in the corporate world, each of them believing that cooking was far too domestic a chore to concern themselves with.

Libby had reorganised the pantry, done three loads of washing and cleaned both bathrooms by the time Cleo finally emerged from her bedroom. Dressed in her pyjamas, with the remnants of last night's mascara smudged under her eyes, Cleo meandered into the lounge room and switched on the TV before collapsing on the couch.

Knowing that any comment made would be taken the wrong way and she would get the inevitable response, 'Mum, chill out! I've studied so hard these past few weeks I just have to veg!', Libby held her tongue. She already knew Cleo intended to laze around the house, treating it like a hotel where Libby was both the maid who picked up after her and room service who provided her with the meals she fancied.

It would be even longer before Brianna surfaced. She favoured watching movies until the early hours during the holidays and rarely surfaced before mid-afternoon. Once again Libby was expected to cater to her offspring's lifestyle choice by keeping the house dark and quiet in the mornings and having an all-day menu at the ready.

Libby wondered where she had gone wrong with her children. Working all the shifts she could had allowed her to provide her daughters with a lifestyle she had only dreamed of as a child. Sure, they had all the material things they needed and wanted and would end up in well-paying careers, but they seemed to lack any kind of drive or ingenuity. She'd given them everything on a plate and as a result they would probably never know the value of hard work or the value of having a dream and working towards it.

Libby was eating a tuna sandwich and reading the paper when her mobile phone rang. Picking it up she hesitated when she saw her colleague Colleen's name on the screen. A call at this hour meant one thing – a fill in shift at the hospital. Normally Libby jumped at the chance to do an extra shift at casual rate, but today she had the pudding to consider. It had to be delivered tomorrow morning, meaning it had to go in the oven this afternoon.

She could ignore the call, but Colleen would continue to ring until she got some kind of response. Sighing, she swiped the screen. 'Hello Col, I'm just—'

Colleen acted like she hadn't heard her. 'Oh Lib, I'm so glad I caught you! Can you please, please come in this afternoon?'

'Oh, Col, no I really can't today. I really am in the middle of something and—'

Having been the shift supervisor for many years, Colleen knew who to target and exactly what to say to get people in to work on their day off. 'Lib, we're up the creek today. Julie put her back out and had to go home, Carmen has got the trots and Anne apparently has some mystery twenty-four-hour virus. Yes, I know, she's probably hung over and we shouldn't condone her taking a sick day for that reason, but the point is she's not here and we're desperate. Remember the health minister is coming this afternoon and the place needs to look like it's running properly even if it isn't. Not to mention the shift bonus for coming in at short notice.'

Sighing, Libby considered her options. As always, she could use the extra cash and with the shift bonus she could get those new shoes she'd been eyeing off. If she put the pudding in the oven now, surely she could trust Cleo to take it out again? An academically gifted young woman who breezed through her university exams should be able to follow simple instructions, right?

Misinterpreting her silence as consent, Colleen started talking again. 'Oh, thanks Lib, we need someone of your calibre today, trust me. See you ASAP.'

'Yes, all right.'

Cleo was still in her pyjamas watching Ellen when Libby poked her head into the lounge room. 'Cleo, I've been called into work and I need you to take the pudding out of the oven for me in two hours' time. You'll need to set the timer on your phone because the one on the oven is broken. And you'll need to video it.'

Cleo nodded absently, more interested in the text message she had just received.

Libby raised her voice a notch. 'Cleo, it's important. This pudding is for a competition, I could win a lot of money. Promise me you'll make sure you get it out exactly on time.'

When she got no response, Libby turned off the TV with the remote.

'Hey!' Cleo looked at her mother for the first time. 'I heard you, get the pudding out of the oven and film it. I'll set my timer. I'm a uni student, Mum, I can follow directions,' she said, flicking the TV back on.

'Great. I'll leave it in your capable hands.'

Cleo was already engrossed in Ellen again. 'Yeah, yeah, I'll take care of it.'

It was so busy at the hospital that Libby didn't have time to text Cleo until seven. Unlike the lightning fast replies she sent her friends, it took Cleo fifteen minutes to respond with a thumbs up. Rolling her eyes, Libby sighed in relief. Even though she'd only decided to enter the competition that morning, it felt like something she really had to do.

It was almost two a.m. when Libby finally got home. The lure of an extra half shift at double time meant she could definitely buy her shoes and maybe a new dress too, just in case she needed it for any official occasions, she thought tiredly, as she let herself in the back door. But now, all she wanted to do was sleep. As soon as she had checked her precious pudding, of course.

Trudging into the kitchen, Libby ignored the food debris on the bench and the sink full of dirty dishes and headed straight for the table, where the diamond pudding sat in all it's glory. She'd really excelled herself this time, she decided, observing how neatly all the layers had come together and how light and airy the sponge top was. When the judges tasted this little beauty, she would be in with a real chance, for sure.

Smiling with pleasure, she turned off the light and headed for the shower.

Completely new to the world of cooking contests, Libby hadn't realised just how long and tedious the judging process was. Along with the other entries, her pudding was sliced and scrutinised by a panel of judges for at least ten minutes before it was even tasted. The revered food critic, Albert Smythe, seemed especially suspicious of the delicate sponge layer, prodding and crumbling it in his fingers. 'And this is definitely hand mixed you say?' he asked, peering over his glasses at Libby.

'Yes, of course. It's the only way I ever make it. You can see on the video I submitted.'

'Hmm,' was Albert's response.

Watching the judges chew each bite slowly and confer in whispers among themselves was excruciating. Suddenly Libby was full of doubt. One of the eggs had been questionable, the milk was slightly out of date…maybe she should never have entered. Gnawing on her thumbnail, Libby was on the verge of slipping into the pub next door for a gin and tonic when she was announced the winner.

Having never sought the limelight before, Libby nevertheless enjoyed her new status as a minor celebrity. Even Cleo and Brianna were happy for her. She'd expected indifference from them and maybe even a lecture about perpetuating gender stereotypes by entering such contests, but they seemed excited, if not a little amused by the result.

'So, the judges really liked it, then?' Cleo asked, stifling a smile as she nudged her sister.

'Yes, they did. They wouldn't have placed it first if they didn't like it, would they?'

'No, they wouldn't, I suppose.'

'You suppose? Don't you believe I'm a good enough cook to win? You certainly don't complain when I serve the pudding up for you.'

'Of course you deserved to win, Mum,' Brianna said, frowning at Cleo. 'We're just interested how the whole contest thing works. And how much money you won too. Maybe we could go on an overseas holiday or something.'

'The cash prize is twenty thousand dollars, most of which will be going on the mortgage.'

Brianna's face fell at this news, but Cleo, the accounting student, nodded approvingly. 'Great idea. You'll save years off the back end.'

'It really is great, Mum. Now what's for dinner?' asked Brianna.

* * * * *

Libby loved her new career in the Delightful Desserts kitchen. A start-up company, they focused on old fashioned cooking, shunning labour-saving devices and selling their own range of aprons, whisks, mixing bowls and wooden spoons. Libby's job was running cooking classes and weekend retreats, teaching people how to enjoy food preparation again. 'When my great-grandmother created this delightful dessert, she thought nothing of the time it took to make it,' Libby would say, as she supervised a room full of men and women carefully hand whipping egg whites and painstakingly assembling the layers together. 'I wouldn't be here today with you all if it wasn't for this pudding.'

Her students nodded in agreement at the sentiment, but Libby wasn't sure if they were all on board with giving up their Thermomixes. She liked to think she'd inspired at least a few of them to embrace the old days, anyway. Besides, seeing her treasured Diamond Pudding in selected boutique food markets was all the reward she needed – even if Delightful Desserts had yet to pay her cash prize. It was a somewhat blurry clause on her contract, with the legal department assuring her these things always took time to iron out completely.

It wasn't just cooking that Delightful Desserts educated Libby in either. Under their mentorship program, she was paired with judge, Albert Smythe, a food critic who'd once written for the defunct Daily Sun. It was Albert who shepherded Libby through her first tumultuous months in her new career – talking her through several crises of confidence and assuring her that her lack of formal qualifications was no barrier to her ongoing success. 'We call it the Masterchef effect,' Albert said, his expression hardening ever so slightly. 'If your product is "discovered" you no longer have to spend years in the trenches hoping for your big break. Not like the old days where chefs had to pay their dues and food critics held much more sway,' he added, his tone suggesting that the old days were, in fact, more to his liking.

Cleo and Brianna made no secret of their dislike for Albert, labelling him creepy and a has-been. While Libby could understand that his penchant for hair oil and garish bow ties might make him come across as creepy, she thought that has-been was unfair. Sure, the advent of the celebrity chef and the internet had seen him drop out of the spotlight, but Albert was still well known in the industry. Why else would Delightful Desserts have snapped him up?

In any case the girls remained somewhat amused by her newfound success in general. While outwardly supportive, Libby sensed they didn't really take the whole thing seriously. To them she was still Mum who cooked and cleaned for them, not a well-regarded chef in the hottest new start up in town. Having just started work experience at a large accounting firm, Cleo had plenty of advice for Libby on how to handle her financial affairs.

'You need to be wary about his job, Mum. It's great you love what you do, and that old-fashioned cooking is on trend now, but people are fickle. What's cool this year won't necessarily be so fab in two years' time,' said Cleo, as she set the table for dinner.

'She's right,' Brianna agreed, pouring them each a glass of wine. 'Delightful Desserts are the innovators, so they will get away with selling overpriced merchandise and hosting expensive classes for a while. But once a few more people jump on the bandwagon the competition heats up. The big shops will start flogging cheap mixing bowls and someone will start putting videos for free on YouTube and then people won't be so willing to part up with their cash.'

'You girls are so cynical,' Libby said, as she served up her succulent roast lamb. 'Is this the thanks I get for sending you to university? To undermine my achievements?'

'We're not undermining, Mum. Just saying be careful. Every new trend dies eventually, it's one of the first things we learned in Intro to Marketing.' Brianna shrugged as if to say, *what can you do?*

'Oh Bri, this isn't about marketing. Traditional Cooking is a real movement and it's here to stay. I will take your financial advice, Cleo, and invest my pennies wisely, but I'm not concerned about my future with Delightful Desserts.'

'All right,' Cleo said, a tad condescendingly Libby thought, as her daughters exchanged one of their annoying knowing glances across the table. 'Maybe keep paying your nursing registration, though, just in case.'

Shaking her head, Libby sat down. 'Oh no, Sweetheart. My nursing days are definitely over.'

Although she never said, 'I told you so', to Cleo, it was immensely satisfying to Libby to witness the continued success of Delightful Desserts. The diamond pudding was as popular as ever and when she was offered directorship of the company six months later, she didn't even mention it to Cleo, not wanting to have to sit through another financial lecture about risk and covering her bases and the like. Sure, she would have to take out a second mortgage, but, as Albert pointed out, the promised returns would well and truly cover her repayments. Now she was finally in a position of financial security, Libby was willing, for the first time in her life, to act on the adage that you have to speculate to accumulate.

As much as she longed to share the news with the girls, Libby held off, wanting to nail down all the details and prove to herself, as much as to her daughters that she was now a successful businesswoman and capable of taking care of her own affairs.

* * * * *

As it turned out, Libby never did get the chance to tell the girls how successfully she was managing her financial affairs. As Brianna predicted, the old-fashioned cooking movement went large scale and Delightful Desserts became a much smaller fish in a very crowded pond. Class numbers plummeted, and merchandise sat on the shelves gathering dust, even at a deeply discounted price. While the Diamond Pudding continued to sell well in its boutique food market niche, it was not enough to sustain the otherwise failing company.

Libby remained hopeful for the first few months, believing Albert's reassurances that things would turn around. It was only when their impending liquidation was the headline story on the news that Libby fully realised just how bad things were.

'You need to get out of there right now, Mum!' Brianna said, her eyes wide as the reporter announced how much the creditors were owed.

Cradling her head in her hands Libby revealed just how deeply she was in and all Brianna could do was hold her as she sobbed.

* * * * *

Cleo and Brianna gave Libby the space she needed to wallow for a couple of days. They didn't try and coax her into joining them for dinner (take away), nor did they deny her requests for ice-cream and chocolate, while she binge watched Netflix. It was only when Colleen rang and offered Libby her old job back that the girls stepped in.

Flicking the TV off, Brianna moved Libby's feet and perched on the end of the couch. 'Are you thinking of going back to the hospital?'

Libby shrugged listlessly. 'What choice do I have? I'll be tied to that place forever, now if I want any chance of paying both the mortgages off. Let's face it, I don't have any formal training in the food industry, and nobody will touch me now after all this.'

'Want to hear another option?'

'There isn't one, Bri.'

'I reckon there is. I've been checking your contracts with Delightful Desserts and although they used your recipe, they never actually had you sign it over to them. A dodgy practice, given they traded on it, but in this case, it has worked out in your favour.'

'Why does that matter if they own it or not? I can't do anything with it now.'

'Cleo and I think you can. You showed the diamond pudding has marketability, so why not go big on it and try for the major supermarkets?'

Smiling sadly, Libby shook her head. 'The big supermarkets only accept things that can be successfully created on a large scale. The time it takes to make the pudding would cancel out their profit margin.'

'Mum, when Great Grandma created that recipe, she had to do everything by hand because she didn't have any appliances. It had to cool for a long time because she had to use an ice box and she had to cook it at a lower heat because she had an unreliable wood stove.'

'How on earth do you know that?'

'Duh, Mum, I googled it. There's a lot of info out there about how to modernise recipes. Have you ever tried using any shortcuts before?'

'No, never. I was taught that I had to follow the recipe *exactly*.'

'So, why don't you try some shortcuts? Then you'll know for sure. And if it works, I can help you pitch it to people of influence. You can be the subject of my marketing thesis.'

Pushing the blanket back that she'd wrapped herself in, Libby sighed. 'All right, Bri, I'll give it a go.'

It felt like sacrilege to pour the ingredients into the Kenwood and to use the hand mixer to beat the egg whites instead of the old whisk, but half an hour in Libby wondered why she had never done it before. The consistency was perfect as she assembled the layers much faster than it would have normally taken. Skipping the room temperature cool down, she instead put the mixture in the freezer for half an hour. Cranking the temperature on the oven she reduced the cooking time by an hour. Libby watched the pudding anxiously as it cooked and examined it suspiciously once it came out of the oven, but outwardly it looked just the same. Waiting just an hour to slice it, rather than the traditional three, Libby was once again amazed at the consistency and taste. It tasted just as good, even better than the old school way. Summoning Cleo and Brianna into the kitchen she had them do a taste test and the consensus was unanimous. The diamond pudding had just been dragged into the twenty first century.

* * * * *

It wasn't quite an overnight success, but within six months the Diamond Pudding Company was born and a year later its namesake was on supermarket shelves all over the country. There was even talk of exporting it to Asia, where it had received rave reviews at a food expo in Hong Kong. Dragging out her grandmother's handwritten recipe books, Libby adapted a further three old-fashioned pudding recipes that would be on supermarket shelves the following year.

Joining in her new enterprise was her former mentor, Albert. True, his fussy but exacting manner could be wearing at times but, on the flip side, his wealth of knowledge helped Libby through the minefield of her first year in business. Of course, Cleo and Brianna warned her that he was only interested in riding on her coattails and had only approached her to keep his own flagging career alive, but Libby believed his passion for her product was genuine.

And, as for her daughters, that was the most amazing thing of all. Taking Albert's advice to employ some proper management staff, Libby had invited both of them to join the company. Realising her plan to take the corporate marketing world by storm by the age of twenty-five was not realistic, Brianna had jumped at the chance to become Marketing Manager. Similarly disillusioned by her role at the ATO, Cleo had happily accepted the Chief Finance Officer position. Libby had to pinch herself sometimes with the realisation her daughters had ended up not only working with her but also in the food industry when neither of them could do much more than boil an egg. What did it matter, though? They did what they were passionate about, leaving her to do the cooking, as she had always done. Who knew that fateful morning she had decided to enter the contest just how all their lives would be transformed?

Libby had even forgiven the Delightful Dessert company for the way they had treated her. While she wouldn't want to relive the experience, it was the catalyst for branching out on her own. Just think what she would have missed if she'd stayed working for them.

*T*he agenda for the weekly staff meeting was long forgotten as Libby, Albert and the girls sat around the board room table. Flicking through the pages of the thick legal document, Brianna shook her head, her face becoming redder by the second. 'Those dirty dogs! I knew they were a dodgy company. It's all right for them to not pay your cash prize, but as soon as you succeed on your own, they stick their grubby hands out!'

'I don't get how they can sue you,' Cleo said.

Libby shrugged listlessly. 'Apparently I wasn't allowed to modernise the recipe after all because I won the contest with it. It was one of the terms and conditions. I suppose I should have read them.'

'Nobody ever does,' said Cleo.

'Be that as it may,' Albert interjected, 'ignorance is not a valid form of defence. I just assumed you had sorted that side of things before you went out on your own. Of course, if I'd known, I would have advised you against it.'

Throwing Albert a dirty look, Brianna held up her hand. 'Just wait a minute. I haven't finished reading this yet. It might not be as bad as we think.'

'Oh, I think you'll find it is, unfortunately,' Albert replied. 'I must say I am relieved that you never offered me shares in the company, after all.'

Jumping to her feet, Cleo jabbed her finger in Albert's direction. 'That's enough out of you! Don't think Brianna and I don't know what you've been up to this whole time, trying to worm your way into *our* family business.'

'*Your* business?' scoffed Albert. 'The one you waltzed into when it was already successful? I don't recall either of you being there for the hard work, for the countless hours of hand holding and reassuring...' His voice trailed off as her realised he may have said too much. 'Not that I minded, of course,' he said. 'But still, if that's the way you feel, then I suppose the family business will have to wear the financial cost all by itself.'

'Oh, yes, how convenient for you,' Cleo snapped.

'Please, let's not fight,' Libby murmured, head bowed as she tried to take in what was happening.

Clasping his hands together, Albert gave them a pitying glance. 'Let me save you all some time. I have read the document from start to finish and it states that the methods used to create the *specific Dessert* entered in the contest cannot be altered for the purposes of large-scale marketing. They have the video of Libby creating her pudding, proving that was how she made it. You've got no comeback from that.'

Upon hearing this Cleo and Brianna sat up straighter. Eyes widening, Cleo glanced over at her sister. 'So, it's how the contest entry was made? The one the judges tasted?'

'Yes,' Albert agreed. 'That's what I said.'

The girls stared at each other, excitement evident in their expressions. 'OMG!' Brianna exclaimed. 'We can totally refute this!'

It was Libby's turn to stare then, eyeing her daughters as if they were crazy. 'What do you mean?'

'Well on the day of the contest, remember you told me to take the pudding out of the oven?' Cleo said.

'Yes, of course I remember. I wasn't sure if you'd actually do it.'

'You were right. I didn't do it. I didn't bother setting my phone timer and I forgot all about the pudding until I smelled it burning. Bri and I freaked out, knowing how important it was and all. I couldn't believe it just slipped my mind like that. Anyway, in desperation we put a help post on this cooking forum and someone said to put it in the mixer, cool it in the freezer and make the oven hotter. To be honest we didn't like our chances of it working out, but we figured we had to try.'

Libby's mouth dropped open. 'So, that pudding I entered was one you two made?'

Cleo and Brianna nodded.

'I can't believe that! How on earth did you make the sponge so perfectly?'

Brianna laughed. 'We totally cheated on the sponge mix. That came from the bakery.'

'I'm flabbergasted,' said Libby, shaking her head. 'I didn't think you girls even knew where the recipe books were, let alone how to operate the mixer.'

'Of course we knew where the recipe books were,' said Cleo, in an offended tone. 'But we did have to google how to use the mixer. And some nice lady in America coached us how to put the layers together.'

Libby gave a knowing smile. 'Well, well, well. You did inherit some of my cooking talents after all. Wonders will never cease. And, of course, that's how you knew the recipe could be modernised.'

'Yep,' agreed Brianna. She and Cleo exchanged a high five.

Albert shook his head. 'That's a very convenient story, and impossible to prove, I'm afraid.'

'Are you kidding?' said Cleo. 'We filmed the whole thing, including the burnt mess I pulled out of the oven. I posted it on Facebook too. It will still be there and on my phone too, of course.'

Albert's face paled. 'What?'

'Sorry, Albert, your little plan just backfired.'

'If you're suggesting for one moment that I was a part of this…'

'I don't have to suggest anything. I know it. How much is your kickback?'

Completely unprepared for Cleo's direct question,

Albert's guilty expression said it all. 'I beg your pardon!' he finally stammered.

Folding her arms slowly and deliberately, Cleo stared him down. 'You've got thirty seconds to resign before Mum sacks you.'

'Now, just a moment,' said Albert. 'I hate to break it to you two little princesses, but your mother has bent my ear on many occasions about how entitled you are. Don't assume she's going to do what you tell her to.'

It was Cleo and Brianna's turn to look outraged as they turned to stare at Libby.

Smirking, Albert shrugged his shoulders. 'Let's just see what Mummy dearest has to say before you go around making ultimatums. She is the boss, after all.'

With all eyes in the room upon her Libby cradled her head in her hands and said nothing.

'Libby?' Albert prompted.

Exhaling loudly Libby finally looked up. 'It's true,' she said. 'I did say you were entitled.'

Both girls opened their mouths to protest but Libby held up her hand to stave off the attack. 'Oh, come on, you two. You know you're entitled but I let you be so that's on me. And, as for you, Albert, you are correct. I am the boss and I second Cleo. You can either resign or be sacked. It's true, the girls weren't around for the ground work and they did get a free ride into a successful company but only I'm allowed to say that, not you. Of all the crimes you've committed here, the biggest one was coming between a mother and her children.'

The Perfect Proposal

*C*lare had never experienced such anger before.

Two weeks on and it was still white hot, bubbling just beneath the surface. She had never realised how all-encompassing anger could be, how it could invade every waking thought and make her muscles tense with no conscious effort. Only when her jaw started to ache did she realise she was clenching it again. It was an automatic reaction now, every time an email or text message arrived, or when she glanced at her mobile and saw the missed call icon. Or even when she just thought about him.

'You should do something you enjoy to distract yourself,' Clare would counsel her clients when they revealed how anger affected their lives.

While it was worthwhile advice, Clare discovered it could certainly be expensive, and after the facial, pedicure and aromatherapy massage last weekend, she decided on the cheaper option of a movie this week.

As she stood in the queue waiting for Cinema 12 to start seating, Clare dived into her handbag for her phone. Glancing at the screen before she switched to mute mode, she raised her eyebrows in surprise. There was nothing from Matt. Maybe he was finally getting the message or maybe it was just a bit early in the night for him to start harassing her.

It was ironic, really. As a health care professional, she spent her days advising others how to deal with their emotions and yet Clare couldn't bring herself to communicate in any way with the man she had recently moved 2000 kilometres for.

She had never considered herself and Matt to be a "perfect couple", but the truth was, they rarely fought. Matt was the epitome of laid back, so much so he was almost horizontal, and Clare prided herself on being calm and level headed. Having spent so much of their early relationship separated by distance they had learnt to make their time together count, which meant not wasting precious moments in conflict.

In hindsight, maybe that was not such a good thing, Clare acknowledged, as she filed into the cinema with the other moviegoers. And, in all fairness, she should probably take the blame for that. Because the truth was, meeting Matt had allowed her to feel organised and efficient for the first time in her life. It had taken some getting used to that she wasn't the one who was running the latest or who had misplaced the plane tickets or the car keys. So, she had always laughed about it, and even encouraged it by insisting she loved him just as he was.

And now it had come back to bite her. What was the old saying – it's all fun and games until somebody loses an eye?

There was being charmingly absent-minded and then there was being just plain careless. And she was the one paying the price.

t took the cab driver a while to find the hall. Although Matt was familiar with certain areas of Melbourne now, others were just a name on a map, like Forest Hill, so he wasn't much help with directions. He had planned to slip in right at the last minute, anyway, but was now actually five minutes late.

Jogging up the concrete steps, Matt paused for a moment to look at the poster advertising tonight's lecture. The diamond ring and bright red text announcing "The Perfect Proposal" had no doubt drawn in plenty of guys looking for some inspiration. Guys like him, who needed a bit of help.

Smiling apologetically at the young woman on the front desk, he extracted a fifty-dollar note from his wallet and handed it over.

She was brisk and efficient. 'There you go, that's twenty dollars change and your ticket. It's already started, so you'll have to sneak in quietly.'

'Sure, no worries,' Matt replied. Slipping his wallet back into his pocket, he started walking towards the door, but hesitated before going in. Turning back, he asked the young woman, 'So have you seen the presentation?'

'Oh, yes!' she enthused. 'It's fabulous.'

'So I've heard,' Matt murmured, reconsidering yet again. Maybe he shouldn't be here? Clare would definitely not approve of him gate crashing her lecture. But, then again, it was a free country and he had paid his admission like everybody else. Besides, he hadn't seen her for three weeks and was starting to get desperate.

The door was old and heavy and almost impossible to sneak through. Inching it open, Matt squeezed through the smallest gap possible. Once inside, he breathed a sigh of relief. The lighting was muted, focusing on the speaker at the lectern, not the audience. There were a couple of spare rows at the back, so it would be a simple matter to just slip into the darkest corner without being noticed.

Gently easing the door closed with only the tiniest click, Matt made his way over to the left, careful to tiptoe on the wooden floor. Unfortunately, however, he didn't notice the music stand that had been placed right at the back of the hall and bumped straight into it, knocking the metal frame to the floor with an almighty clang.

It was one of those horrible moments where everybody in the room turned and stared, including Clare, whose words he had so rudely interrupted. Matt's breath caught in his throat as he and the woman he loved so much locked eyes for just a second before she looked away, clearly annoyed.

Sinking down into a chair, Matt buried his face in his hands. She was going to kill him.

Matt had known he wanted to marry Clare fairly early into their relationship. After meeting her, he *finally* understood why he had never felt even the slightest urge to take the plunge with any of the other women he had dated, despite the fact that several of them had made their expectations very clear.

Even though his dad had been dead almost twenty years now, Matt could clearly remember the advice he had given him on his eighteenth birthday. Out for their first official drink together, Matt had literally cried into his beer because his first serious girlfriend had just dumped him.

'If this is what love feels like, I don't want it,' he had sniffled.

'Matthew, that's how you tell the real thing. She *won't* make you feel like this,' his father had reassured him.

And in all honesty, no other woman had broken his heart in the interim; it was always he who backed away. Not because he was trying to avoid commitment, rather because Matt knew it just wasn't the *real thing* his dad had talked about.

Of course people assumed if you were single and in your mid-thirties then there must be a *reason*. It was often the pivotal question women asked on a first date.

'You seem like such a nice guy – why are you still single?'

'Because I haven't met the right woman yet,' he would reply.

It was a simple and honest answer but was often met with scepticism.

Matt could understand that to a point. After all, if you met the love of your life when you were young, you probably assumed love came easily to everybody. But he knew that just wasn't the case.

His mother thought it was because he was too comfortable in his carefree bachelor lifestyle.

The women at work told him he was being too picky.

His cousin, Darryl, told him it was because he had never tried internet dating.

Matt knew it was for none of those reasons and held firm on waiting for the real thing, although he had to admit there were moments of doubt, as he watched all of his friends and then his younger sister get hitched and start reproducing.

But then, just when he was wondering if, in fact, there was something seriously wrong with him, Michael Buble's words had hit home. Clare had "come out of nowhere and into his life" and he understood what his dad had been talking about. Unlike many men, he was comfortable with the idea of getting married. Unfortunately, he just had a problem with proposing.

Even if Matt didn't know and love Clare he would have been impressed with the evening. Full of practical advice delivered in Clare's trademark no-nonsense style, it was actually kind of fun. He had little doubt that most of the men there had been ordered, or at least coerced, into going by their girlfriends or partners, but most seemed to be enjoying it and interacting, which was obviously the whole idea.

'All right, now we're at the critical point,' Clare announced, back at the lectern after mingling with various groups during the last discussion time. 'The proposal.'

She paused dramatically, allowing the words to permeate around the room.

'The proposal is the big moment, right?'

She was answered by a barrage of nods and some mumbled yeses.

'It's the moment that your other half puts all the emphasis on.'

More nods.

'Would you say it sets the tone for a marriage?'

At least half the audience nodded.

'Do you feel like it has to be *perfect*?'

A barrage of nods this time.

Clare sighed dramatically. 'Oh dear! Well, if that's what you believe, I predict that both you and your beloved are in for some disappointment.' With that she raised her eyebrows and nodded meaningfully, locking eyes with Matt in a way that made him feel very nervous.

'Of course, social media has a lot to answer for,' Clare continued. 'Fifty or even twenty years ago, most couples only shared details of their engagement with their closest friends and family, but these days it's all over Facebook and YouTube. I get it, I know that puts you guys under a lot of pressure.'

Pausing, she met Matt's gaze again and this time he saw the hint of a smile on her face. He immediately slunk down in his seat, realising with a jolt that she was going to somehow involve him. What an idiot he was for coming! Please don't, he pleaded silently. Please, please, please don't make me do something.

Alas, his pleas remained unanswered as Clare resumed her speech. 'Gentlemen, I believe there is nothing like a true story to illustrate a point and I'm sure among you there is somebody who would just love to share their own experience, good or bad, with the group. Having read through your questionnaires, I know there are many case studies we could discuss.'

Unsurprisingly, almost every head bowed at that point, to avoid making eye contact with Clare, everybody else as desperate as Matt to avoid being singled out.

'Oh, come on, gents, it's not that bad! How about I nominate someone? Yes, that's a good idea. Let's see, hmmm, what about you sir, in the very back row?'

Matt kept his eyes down in the hope Clare would choose somebody else, but of course she didn't.

'Come on now, sir, yes, I can still see you – black hair, green hoodie. I'll just send the roving microphone down to you.'

Matt slowly raised his eyes and shook his head, but only as a token gesture. Like it or not, he was about to bare his soul to the world, or at least to a room full of strangers.

* * * * *

Even though breakfast service at the Windsor started at seven o'clock, the dining room was still quiet when Matt arrived just after eight. It didn't surprise him, though, in fact it was one of the things he had come to expect from Melbourne. It took longer for the day to get rolling down here, unlike Queensland where everyone tended to be up and about early. He didn't consider it a bad thing, just one of those little observations you make about different places.

Matt had decided it had a lot to do with climate. Take this

morning, for example. Upon looking out the window, he noted it was a cool, overcast morning. By eight in the morning in Brisbane in late spring, you pretty much knew what how the day was going to turn out. Not so in Melbourne, though. Melbourne didn't hit her straps until mid-afternoon, with the late afternoon generally being the hottest part of the day. The people were similar. Not too many ventured out early, but as the day wore on, they gradually emerged, doing most of their socialising in the afternoon or evening.

The waiter's voice brought him back to the present. 'Table for one, sir?'

Matt sighed deeply. 'Yeah,' he answered forlornly. 'Table for one.'

Although he had initially considered himself too depressed to eat much, Matt still managed to put away a two-egg omelette, three rashers of bacon, two sausages, toast and coffee. Patting his mouth with a monogrammed linen napkin, he took in his luxurious surroundings and tried to be enthusiastic about it. After all it wasn't every day he ate breakfast at The Windsor or stayed in the exclusive Victorian Suite. In fact, it was the first time he ever had.

'Cheer up, sir, it might never happen.'

Matt looked up to see a waiter with a coffee pot.

'You look like you won the lotto and lost your ticket,' the man said, leaning over to refill Matt's cup.

'I think that might have been less depressing.' Matt smiled wanly.

'Oh dear,' the waiter said. Around sixty with greying curly hair, he was as lean as a greyhound and had a kind face that invited the sharing of confidences. His name tag read Barry.

Realising how pathetic he sounded, Matt shook his head. 'Sorry, this was supposed to be a really awesome weekend and it's turned out the exact opposite. No offense to your beautiful hotel, of course.'

'None taken. Obviously it's something pretty major if The Windsor can't work its charm on you.'

'Oh yeah, it's major all right.'

Looking at his watch, Barry glanced at Matt thoughtfully. 'Tell you what, my shift finishes in ten minutes and I've got nothing on this morning. You know Pelligrinis?'

'Yeah, of course.'

'Meet me there in an hour. We'll have some decent coffee and you can tell me what's on your mind.'

'For real?'

'Sure. What's the worst that can happen? I could make you even more depressed than you are already?'

With nothing better to do and his flight home not until five, Matt nodded his agreement. 'All right, why not?'

Fortified with a double espresso, Matt told Barry his sad tale. 'I'm actually supposed to be celebrating my engagement this morning,' he said.

Barry took a sip of his own espresso. 'Oh, I see. She said no, huh? Even after you treated her to the Victorian Suite? That's harsh and extremely expensive.'

Matt shook his head vehemently. 'No, hell no. If that had happened, I think I'd be suicidal.'

'Right,' Barry said slowly, raising his right eyebrow enquiringly. 'So, something else catastrophic happened?'

'No, I wouldn't say catastrophic, exactly,' Matt mumbled. 'More like a comedy of errors, culminating in me being here alone while my girlfriend is back up in Queensland.'

'Listen, Matt, you've dangled the carrot here. I need some details or I'll die of curiosity.'

'Righto, I'll start at the beginning. My girlfriend, Clare, is from Melbourne, I'm from Brisbane, well I live on the Gold Coast now, but you get the picture.'

Barry nodded.

'Anyway, long story short, Clare moved up to Brisbane about six months ago after we long distanced it for a year. She still works down here one week a month and her parents still have a place here, so we're in Melbourne a lot, you know.'

'Sounds like a good deal, with Queensland's weather and Melbourne's culture.'

Matt nodded. 'Something like that. Anyway, Clare's a psychologist, you see, and although she never makes me feel like she's analysing my behaviour, I wanted to show her how much she means to me by orchestrating an amazing proposal.'

'A very noble ambition if I ever heard one. I guess that's where The Windsor comes in, then?'

'Yep. Melbourne is still really special to her and I wanted to take her to the grandest place here.'

'Well, that's The Windsor all right.'

'Anyway, Clare's working down here next week so the plan was to come down for the weekend. She couldn't get a frequent flier flight until yesterday arvo, but I came down on Friday night. I told her I was catching up with a uni mate but it was really to get myself organised.'

'Righto.'

'I booked in, got everything sorted and then she rings at three o'clock to say her work schedule has changed and she's not coming until Wednesday.'

'Oh, and I guess you couldn't make a big song and dance about it because you didn't want to arouse her suspicions, right?'

'Uh huh.'

'Well, it's a bummer all right and I know it's a lot of money to spend, but can't you just reschedule?'

'I don't know. It feels kind of like the opportunity has passed. I mean after all that effort and we couldn't even end up in the same city on the same day? Maybe it's not meant to happen because we're such different people.'

'Different in what way?'

'Clare is really successful in her career. Besides counselling people she's got a talkback radio slot back in Brissie and she's becoming a big name on the corporate speaking circuit.'

'Wow. And what do you do?'

'I'm a journalist for a travel magazine.'

'Nothing wrong with that. In fact I imagine you get lots of perks.'

'Yep, definitely. How do you reckon I afforded to stay at the Windsor?'

Barry laughed. 'I must admit you didn't really fit the bill of our average clientele. Not that we don't welcome every guest, of course.'

'Of course,' Matt echoed, with a smile.

Barry shook his head. 'Is that all you're worried about, that she's more career focused?'

'It's not just her career, she's got her life totally sorted out and I've always just taken it as it comes. I've been told I've got a bit of a Peter Pan complex.'

'Do you think that's necessarily a bad thing?'

'Maybe.'

'Come on, Matt, plenty of couples are opposites. Has she ever asked you to change?'

'No, she'd never do that.'

'Well there you go, you've got nothing to fear.'

Matt took his last sip of espresso. 'Yeah, I guess you're right.'

Matt contemplated Barry's words as he mooched around

Melbourne for the day. He had come to love the city and had even spent three months working there. The weather was the killer, a Queensland boy through and through, he just couldn't acclimatise to the harsh winters.

Usually he and Clare had a great time on the monthly weekend visit, whether it was just relaxing at home, taking in an AFL game (she loved the AFL, he had come to kind of understand it but would always be a League man), hanging in the city or visiting the art gallery, it was just fun being together.

It wasn't like he had never been down there without her either. He had made some friends of his own in Melbourne and there was always someone from Clare's extended family to visit. But today Melbourne just seemed cold and empty and he couldn't wait to head back home.

Maybe it just wasn't meant to happen in Melbourne, he decided, as he stowed his backpack in the overhead locker. Flying with Jetstar so often, he had become a master at packing light, so he didn't have to pay for checked luggage.

His phone beeped just as he sat down. Reading Clare's message, he smiled. "Travel safe - I'll come and pick you up. Missed you heaps xxxx"

Matt flicked a love heart emoji back in reply, then switched to flight mode and shoved the phone in his pocket, feeling his mood lift long before the plane took off.

* * * * *

Matt debriefed the situation with his best mate, Liam, and another friend, Tom. It was a more civilised chat than he had envisaged. His initial thought had been a decent pub session, but given that his mates were married with kids, the best he could arrange on short notice was a Saturday morning takeaway coffee in the park at Rainbow Bay. Tom had a brief window before he had to pick up his children from swimming training and Liam had enlisted his twin ten-year-old nieces Anna and Belle to babysit his ten-month-old daughter, Milly, so he could talk unfettered for a while. At least he hadn't brought his high-spirited, mixed breed puppy, Caesar, with him. As loveable as the dog was, he went crazy in public places, requiring all Liam's attention to keep him under control.

'So, you reckon it really was just bad timing?' Matt asked, after he finished speaking.

'Yeah, buddy,' Liam assured him. 'There's always variables you can't control, especially when it involved planes and travel.'

'I guess so,' Matt sighed.

'Come on, mate,' Tom said, 'it's not like you didn't put the effort in.'

'Totally,' agreed Liam. 'Although, I must say, I'm pretty amazed you came up with The Windsor.'

'Now I know for sure you never read my articles. Clearly you didn't see my feature on The Windsor last month. I interviewed a woman who organises romantic getaway packages and she arranged the whole thing for me.'

'Okay, busted,' Liam smiled sheepishly. 'I'm just a bit behind on my reading at the moment.'

'Yeah, you and Clare both. It was lucky on this occasion, though.'

'Yep, you might have lost a few points for originality,' Liam agreed.

'Maybe I dodged a bullet?' Matt said. 'Maybe Clare subconsciously sensed it was coming and backed off.'

Tom shook his head. 'Are you kidding? Clare is a woman in her thirties, the probability she wants to get married is pretty high. Has she ever indicated that she doesn't believe in marriage?'

'No, definitely not.'

'Well, there you go then,' said Tom.

'Yeah,' Liam agreed. 'Mate you've been together for eighteen months and Clare isn't backwards and coming forwards. She would have told you if marriage wasn't on the agenda.'

'That's true. But do you think it matters that I don't have a lot to offer her? I was supposed to be a successful novelist by the time I was thirty.' Matt took his last sip of coffee.

Lying down on the grass, Liam closed his eyes. 'Yeah, that's right,' he chuckled. 'You're only six years behind schedule. How is the brilliant, as-yet-unnamed, book going, anyway?'

Matt crushed his empty cup and threw it at Liam's head. 'It's going about as well as that rusty, dilapidated Kombi van you've been restoring for the past decade.'

'Hey, low blow! It's really hard to get parts.'

The conversation was interrupted by the sounds of bickering. 'Uncle Liam!' Anna was shouting, 'Tell her it's my turn to change the nappy.'

'They're fighting about changing a nappy?' Tom asked.

Liam smiled wryly, his eyes still closed. 'They get a five-dollar bonus for the gross ones. Sometimes I think they secretly feed her prunes just to make a profit.'

Belle ran over to where they were sitting and stuck her hands on her hips. 'Uncle Liam, it's MY turn!' she announced.

Liam sat up, stuck his hand in his pocket and extracted a handful of two-dollar coins. 'How about you share it for eight dollars?'

Belle considered for a moment, then scooped the change into her hand. 'All right,' she agreed and ran off.

Tom checked his watch and took his last sip of coffee.

'Okay, gotta head, guys, but keep me in the loop, hey?'

'There's a loop?' Matt asked.

'Yep, you've involved us now,' Tom said.

'Uh huh,' Liam agreed. 'Run your next idea by us first and we'll green light it for you.'

'Yeah, we've been there, done that. Consider us the voice of experience,' said Tom, gathering his phone and keys.

Matt raised an eyebrow. 'No offence, guys, but I'm thinking next level here.'

'We can do next level, but right now I'm outta here,' said Tom, waving as he walked away.

'Lucky for you, I've got a bit more time to spare,' said Liam. 'Let's thrash out some ideas for attempt number two.'

* * * * *

Matt paused for a moment and met Clare's eyes for the first time since he had started speaking.

She was all business. 'So,' she said, 'you were game to try again?'

'Um, yeah, I was. Let's face it, bad timing affects everybody at some stage.'

'Yes, it certainly can,' Clare agreed giving him one of her best cool stares.

'And it wasn't like the intention wasn't there.'

'That's true.'

'Uh, I suppose you want me to keep going with the story, then?' Matt murmured, desperate to break the tension.

'Oh, definitely, we'd all love to hear what happened next.'

'All right,' Matt agreed, then cleared his throat and started talking again.

* * * * *

Although he hadn't been doing surf patrol as long as Liam or Tom, Matt was still an established member of his local surf club. So, once the renewed proposal plan was hatched, it wasn't too difficult to arrange a ride for he and Clare in the rescue helicopter early one morning before patrol began.

A little more difficult to arrange was a careful configuration of words on white poster board up at Point Danger. Fortunately, Liam's nine nieces and nephews (plus a few of their friends) had willingly agreed to be the poster holders once he promised them all a season pass to Wet and Wild. It was just as well that Liam came from a big family and that Matt could get a 70% discount on theme park passes through work.

Matt tried to keep his expression normal as he and Clare waited to board the helicopter at Coolangatta. Well aware that he was liable to break into a stupid goofy grin if he concentrated too much on what was ahead, he leant in to hug Clare so she couldn't read his face.

'Wow, this is very nice,' she said, hugging him back. 'May I ask what inspired you to arrange all this?'

'Does there have to be a reason?' he replied, holding her a little tighter.

Clare gave him a little squeeze and then gently pulled away. 'No, of course not. I was just curious.'

'You always said you would love to have a ride in a helicopter. I mentioned it to one of the pilots ages ago and he finally got around to arranging it for me.'

'And I've accused you of not listening to me.'

'Yes, you have. Quite unfairly as it turns out.'

Clare punched him playfully on the arm. 'Yeah, I know, I'm such a nag.'

They grinned at each other companionably.

'Ah, look, here comes our ride,' Matt announced, as the

chopper came into view. Now the moment was upon him, he was hit with some serious adrenaline. Suddenly his heart began to pound so fiercely that he was sure Clare must be able to hear it.

Helping his fiancée-to-be inside, he gave the pilot a surreptitious thumbs up and climbed in after her.

Matt had instructed the pilot to undertake his normal patrol sweep of the Gold Coast beachfront, finishing with a circle over Point Danger. Liam was ready on the ground to co-ordinate the posters. They had practised it endlessly in his yard and had the timing down to split second precision.

Clare clutched Matt's hand excitedly as they lifted off and followed the sweeping coast down towards Surfer's Paradise. It really was a stunning day and the sight of the rolling surf gleaming in the morning sun was so beautiful that Matt himself got caught up in it, forgetting for just a second the purpose behind the ride. This alone was enough to score him some serious brownie points, never mind the proposal.

The pilot caught Matt's eye and raised one eyebrow enquiringly, as he swung the helicopter around to head back south. Matt gave an almost imperceptible nod in response. In his opinion, all women were ridiculously perceptive, but Clare was even more so. He felt she was several steps ahead of him at every turn. Just once, he wanted to totally surprise her.

The adrenaline kicked back in as they neared Coolangatta. Sneaking a glance at Clare, Matt's stomach flipped like it used to on the old Thunderbolt rollercoaster at Dreamworld.

'Oh look, there's Point Danger,' Clare said, pointing into the distance.

'Great spot,' the pilot chipped in through his headset.

Matt and Clare both nodded in agreement, before turning to smile at each other. They loved spending time up there, which was precisely why Matt had picked the spot.

'Oh, wow,' Clare said.

Act cool, Matt told himself before answering in what he hoped was a calm voice. 'What's going on down there?'

Clare shook her head. 'I'm not sure, but there's definitely something happening.'

Matt worked hard to conceal his grin, but he didn't really need to. Clare was too transfixed with what was happening on the ground.

'Oooooh,' she murmured, clasping a hand over her mouth.

Not wanting to be obvious, Matt hadn't yet looked at the ground. Taking Clare's hand, he squeezed it tight. 'What do you reckon?'

Clare's eyes were still on the ground. 'I honestly don't know.'

Matt was back on The Thunderbolt again, but this time he was trapped on the top of the first loop, his feet dangling and his chest compressed hard against the harness. This surely must be one of the worst moments of his life.

'What do you mean you don't know?' he rasped.

Clare still hadn't looked at him. 'I mean I can't work out what's going on. There's a big group of kids running around like crazy things, some are holding pieces of paper I think and others seem to have thrown theirs away ...'

'WHAT?' Matt lurched over to Clare's window and peered out. There was indeed a scene of bedlam on the ground. All fifteen of the children were spread over a twenty-metre radius, some huddling together, others weaving in and out of the crowd that had gathered. Many of the pieces of carefully painted cardboard lay discarded on the ground, while others had been picked up by the wind that often hovered over the Point. Matt watched helplessly as a W and the question mark sailed over the edge of the cliff and down into the surf below.

Slumping back in his seat, Matt shook his head in disbelief. What the hell?

Clare was still wrapped up in the happenings below. 'You're never going to believe this, Babe, but Liam is down there.'

'What are the chances?' Matt mumbled.

'He'll be able to give us all the details. I can't wait! You know how well Liam can tell a story.'

'Oh yeah,' Matt replied darkly. 'He's got a lot of explaining to do.'

When he awoke from his drunken slumber the next morning, Matt was sure he would never eat again. But, as always, by the time lunch rolled around, he was in serious need of some grease and Maccas fit the bill. He had also finally gotten hold of Liam and pinned him down to a meeting time, once again in a park, as Liam's wife, Hayley, was at work. It seemed to Matt that half his social life revolved around parks these days but there were certainly worse places to be than on the foreshore at Coolangatta on a balmy Sunday.

Surprisingly, Liam was already there when he arrived.

'Hey,' Matt mumbled sourly.

'Hey, mate,' Liam replied, much more upbeat. 'I'll grab the food if you like.'

'Yep.'

'Cool. See you over near the swings in a sec,' Liam replied. 'Oh, and can you keep an eye on the kids for me?' he added, as he disappeared across the road.

Matt shook his head. Typical Liam. He loved the guy like a brother, but sometimes he could willingly kill him. Spying Anna and Belle playing with Milly, he found a spot in the shade and lay down on the grass.

The tantalising smell of a Big Mac roused him out of a semi-doze about ten minutes later. Struggling to a sitting position, he accepted the brown paper bag from Liam, noticing that Tom was there too.

'Bumped into Tombo in the queue,' Liam said, plonking himself down near Matt.

Sure you did, thought Matt but didn't argue the point. If the situation was reversed, he would probably seek out moral support too.

'Yeah, I was glad to have an alternative to eating in,' Tom said, choosing his own patch of grass. 'It's just not the same since Macca's moved. It used to be so awesome to wander into the old place soaking wet with sandy feet and kick back in the outside eating area.'

'I'm hearing ya.' Liam unwrapped his Quarter Pounder and waved to the kids.

Tom peeled the paper off his own Big Mac. 'So, Matty, major bummer about yesterday, hey?'

'I'll say,' Matt agreed, shooting Liam a hateful look.

'So…?' Tom enquired, ripping his bag down the side and extracting a handful of fries.

'I'm waiting for our buddy Liam here to tell me all,' replied Matt. 'How our carefully crafted fool proof plan crashed and burned so badly.'

'I'm not sure you could attribute it to just one thing,' Liam said, before shoving a huge chunk of burger in his mouth.

'It never is just one thing with you, mate. So stop stalling and start talking.' Matt stared his friend down.

'Okay, fine. On Friday night I was up late tracking the cyclone up north.' A meteorologist by trade, Liam had an observatory/office on his property. 'Losing track of time as I sometimes do, I fell asleep. No biggie, usually, but Milly is getting a new tooth and had a bad night. Meaning Hayley had an even worse night.'

Holding his hands out in a questioning manner, Matt raised an eyebrow. 'I'm sympathetic towards both Milly and Hayley but I'm still not sure what that's got to do with my second failed proposal.'

'Damage control was required on a very limited time frame. I got Mum to take Milly, but I had to bring Caesar with me so Hayles could go back to bed.'

Matt shook his head as the penny dropped. 'You brought the dog?'

'I had to. And, yes, before you ask, he was on the lead.'

'Yet he still managed to create havoc?'

'I tied him up but somehow he got loose. You know Caesar, he loves to play, but he can be a little bit…'

'Completely out of control in a crowd?' Matt said.

'I was going to say rambunctious.'

Tom nodded. 'And the pieces slowly come together.'

'I tried to calm him down but by that stage a few other dogs had gotten involved. The kids started screaming, the letters got all mixed up, nobody was listening…' Liam bowed his head for a moment before giving his friend a sheepish glance. 'I really am sorry, Matt. It had all the makings of an awesome proposal.'

'Didn't it just?' Matt wasn't quite ready to forgive and forget just yet.

'At least Clare didn't realise what was going on,' said Tom. 'As far as she was concerned you gave her a bucket list experience. There's your silver lining.'

'That's right,' agreed Liam eagerly. 'We could do it again.'

Shaking his head, Matt scrunched up his food wrappers. 'No, too many variables. Not to mention major suspicion when I arrange another helicopter ride. Thanks anyway, guys, but I think this whole situation is outside your scope. I need to go to a higher authority.'

* * * * *

'Well,' said Clare, 'that's a very unfortunate turn of events.'

'Tell me about it,' Matt sighed. 'I seem to attract more than my fair share of them.'

'And did this second failed attempt make your reconsider?'

'Well, yeah, of course. I mean one bout of bad luck could happen to anybody, but two seemed like I was barking up the wrong tree.'

'So, you gave up, then?'

Matt shook his head. 'No, I didn't. As much as I was pretty devoed that I'd stuffed up twice, I still wanted to do it right.'

'By right, you mean perfect?'

'I guess I do – or did.'

'All right, then, don't keep us in suspense, let's hear what happened next.'

* * * * *

Matt's sister, Elizabeth, looked up from the pastry she was rolling out. 'I reckon neutral ground's the go,' she announced.

His other sister, Jill, nodded. 'Yeah, great idea!' she agreed, as she sliced up a Granny Smith apple.

'What?' Matt asked drowsily, adjusting his reclined position on the couch. For such a little guy, his eighteen-month-old nephew, Drew, could be heavy when he was asleep. With Clare in Newcastle for yet another speaking engagement, he was at a loose end *and* in need of a decent feed. Given that his mother was away on a trip to New Zealand, he had invited himself over to Elizabeth's place for Sunday lunch. As it turned out Liz's husband was at work, so Jill tagged along too. Faced with his super inquisitive younger siblings, who knew him too well, it hadn't taken long for the story to come out.

'You should propose on neutral ground. Melbourne didn't work and neither did Coolangatta. Maybe it was because there was too much of each of you invested in those places.'

Matt was still trying to get comfortable with the sleeping child on his chest. 'Or maybe it was because my best mate couldn't control his crazy dog.'

Gathering up the apple peelings, Jill dropped them in the compost bucket. 'Aww, don't say that about Caesar, he's so cute!'

'I never said he wasn't cute, just crazy in a crowd. Typical Liam to end up with the most hyperactive rescue dog at the shelter. Like attracts like, I guess.'

Elizabeth finished filling the apple pie and lay the pastry over the top. 'Don't be so hard on Liam, you know his heart's in the right place,' she said, as she crimped the edges.

'Yeah,' Jill agreed. 'He's a sweetheart.'

'I wouldn't go that far,' Matt grumbled.

Elizabeth put the pie in the oven and waddled over to the recliner. Lowering herself into it, she patted her heavily pregnant belly and looked over at her big brother. 'Don't give up, Matty. You are Clare are great together. Besides that, we love her too and desperately want her as our sister-in-law.'

'Yeah,' echoed Jill, moving Matt's feet and plonking down on the end of the couch.

'I reckon Dad would have liked her,' Matt said.

The girls nodded their agreement, casting their eyes to the framed photo Elizabeth had on the wall. They still missed him every day.

'Well, speaking of Dad, I know he'd be telling you to give it another go,' Jill said.

'He definitely would,' Elizabeth agreed.

'Yeah, I know,' Matt sighed.

They all glanced at the TV, where a documentary about Australia's most expensive real estate was screening. Momentarily transfixed by a mansion overlooking Bondi Beach, Jill suddenly sat up straight and slapped Matt on the leg. 'That's it!' she exclaimed.

'What's it?' Matt scowled, rubbing his stinging flesh.

'Sydney!'

'What about it?' Elizabeth asked, looking at the TV again.

'It's right in the middle between Coolangatta and Melbourne and there's no emotional attachment there for either of you, right?'

'No, we've never actually been there together.'

'Perfect!' Jill declared, reaching for her iPhone.

'It *is* a great idea,' Elizabeth said, smiling encouragingly at Matt.

'You really think so?'

'Yes,' Jill said. 'Leave it to me and Liz and we'll arrange something super special.'

Drew woke up then, opening one eye cautiously and stretching lazily. Seeing Matt, he gave him a full faced grin. Matt smiled in return and held up his hand for a high five. 'Hey, Buddy,' he said, 'Let's hope third time's the charm.'

* * * * *

It was a perfect Sydney summer's day. There wasn't a cloud in the sky and although Matt realised it was probably his imagination, it seemed to be a particularly gorgeous shade of blue. As did the water in the harbour. Dozens of boats bobbed on the sparkling surface, while the ferries chugged steadily over their familiar routes. Sydney really was a beautiful city and today she was showing herself in all her glory.

Matt had to give it to his sisters. They had really come up trumps. Timing the long weekend to coincide with a prestigious conference at the Intercontinental Hotel, where Clare was one of the keynote speakers, they had arranged tickets for a sold-out theatre production at the Opera House, VIP passes to a red carpet movie premiere at Fox Studios and had somehow got them onto the set of *Home and Away* (although Clare denied watching it, everybody knew that she did). But, getting them their own private area on the observation deck at Centrepoint Tower, was the icing on the cake. How they had done it, Matt did not know, but he wasn't one to look a gift horse in the mouth.

Clare was a little unsure about being in the roped off space. 'It says it's for a private function,' she said, her eyes darting nervously around.

Matt took her hand and gently dragged her closer to the window. 'It's fine. There's nobody around.'

'Yeah, but—'

'No buts. They'll tell us to move if they want to.'

'All right, maybe just for a while. It's amazing to have our own little space, isn't it?'

'Oh yeah, absolutely.'

'This has been such a great trip. I can't believe all the stuff we've done. It's like a big celebration, but I'm not sure of the occasion.'

'Is that right?' Matt replied.

Clare eyed him curiously. 'Yes, that's right.'

Meeting her gaze, Matt tried to look as normal as possible, but was sure his face would give him away. 'The occasion is that I love you and I wanted you to be totally relaxed before your big speech tomorrow.'

Clare dropped his hand and planted both palms on her face. 'Oh, man, the speech!' she murmured. 'I can't believe I haven't practised it once since we've been here.'

'You'll be fine. It's been good for you to have a break from it. You can go over it tonight.'

Clare dropped her hands and looked at Matt. 'You really think I can do it?'

'You know you can. Think of all the other speeches you've done. You're a natural.'

'Yeah, but this is the big one. It's a huge audience with heaps of international delegates, not to mention that it's a really complex topic.'

Matt hugged her tight. 'It doesn't matter, you'll still nail it.'

Clare returned the hug. 'Well, how lucky am I to have my own personal speechwriter?'

'Very lucky.'

They stood arm in arm for a moment watching the city bustle beneath them. Matt closed his eyes for a second and surreptitiously took a deep breath. Taking Clare's hand, he tried to decide whether or not to go down on one knee.

'We'll have to go to the computer room and print it out when we get back,' Clare said, as she gave his hand a little squeeze. 'Lucky you had it saved on your memory stick.'

'Memory stick?'

'Come on, Matt. Don't muck around. You know how important this is to me.'

Matt's blood turned to ice as he realised what he had done. Running very late for their flight, he had told Clare not to bother going back to her work to pick up her laptop and the printed copy of her speech as he had it saved on his memory stick. And he did. The only problem was that the memory stick was in the centre console of Liam's car. The car he had dropped them off in before heading off to go camping, in an area with no phone reception.

Matt's audible gasp spoke volumes. 'I left it in the car,' he mumbled.

'Yeah, right. I've fallen for enough of your other pranks not to believe that.'

Matt hesitated, wondering if he could somehow get a message to Liam.

Clare studied his face for a second, then took a step back and looked at him, wild eyed. 'Tell me you're kidding.'

'I'm such an idiot! I put it in there so I wouldn't lose it.'

'Matthew, they are paying me a huge amount of money to deliver a half hour address tomorrow. You assured me I didn't need my laptop and now you've just casually remembered you didn't bring the memory stick. I can't believe you! You're so irresponsible and lackadaisical! You never take anything seriously!'

'Yeah, I do! You know I do! I am so, so sorry!' Matt babbled. 'I'll rewrite it for you, we've got time.'

'We can't rewrite it without all the stats! You can't just talk in general terms about the incidence of bipolar disorder in the community. Besides it's got all the references to other authors, I can't just regurgitate all that at will!'

'Well we can get someone to go to your office.'

'No, we can't! I'm the only one with weekend access, the fob is in my handbag.'

Matt had never seen Clare look that angry. Her normally friendly, open face was a dangerous shade of red and her green eyes looked like they were ready to shoot sparks. Desperately, he tried to console her. 'There must be something we can try,' he said, willing his brain to come up with a magical solution.

Clare shook her head vehemently. 'No, there isn't. You have totally screwed up one of the most important moments of my career. I don't even want to look at you right now.'

With that she stalked off in the direction of the lift.

Matt watched her go. He wanted to follow her, calm her down and try and come up with some crazy way out of the dilemma. Clare was always saying that problems were lessons in disguise. Yet, he was struck with the most intense inertia he had ever experienced. His legs actually felt heavy and the roped off area seemed to have developed into some kind of weird force field that was holding him captive.

Leaning forward on his hands, Matt peered out the window again. Was it just him or had the sky clouded over? Far below, the water looked choppy now and there was some kind of traffic snarl in Pitt Street. How the hell had he botched yet another proposal?

This wasn't just some silly hurdle, Matt realised. It was a clear sign, a divine tap on the shoulder. He and Clare were obviously not meant to get married.

End of story.

* * * * *

Matt paused, acutely aware of the silence in the room. Nobody was fidgeting or shuffling in their chairs. They were all focused on him. It was hard to read the different expressions. Some seemed genuinely sympathetic and were silently telling him, "I'm feeling your pain, buddy." Others looked relieved, perhaps interpreting that they were right in not having taken the proposal leap. And the final group were fighting to hold back their laughter, reassuring themselves at least they weren't *that* inept.

Clare cut back in then, skilfully presenting him with yet

another question. 'So, Matt, after three strikes you must have definitely felt like you were out, right?'

Matt didn't look her in the eye. He couldn't. He had already embarrassed himself enough for one night. 'Yes, absolutely.'

'Yet, at the same time, these experiences must have taught you something, surely?'

Matt cleared his throat. 'Um, they taught me that I was either the unluckiest guy in the world or that I really sucked at proposing.'

'Anything a bit more insightful, perhaps?'

'Um, well, I was going on what other people considered the ideal proposal to be, instead of doing my own thing.'

'Yes, that's true, you should always follow your own instincts. But how else do you think you were subconsciously sabotaging yourself?'

Running his hands through his hair, Matt exhaled sharply. Wow, she was really making him pay for turning up uninvited. 'I was trying too hard to conjure up "perfection",' he replied, holding up his fingers in air quotes.

'Ah, *perfection*. Why did you think you needed perfection?' Clare asked. 'Didn't you know that your girlfriend loved you unconditionally?'

'I guess I didn't.'

'How so?'

Matt sighed. 'Deep down I was scared that I wasn't good enough for her.'

Clare turned her attention back to the audience. 'And this, gentlemen, is the problem. You get so wrapped up in what you think is the perfect proposal, that you forget about the marriage – which is what you should be focused on. Matt here should have resolved the issue he had of not feeling worthy by talking to his partner, or a counsellor, instead of challenging himself to an elaborate proposal to try and bolster his worthiness within their relationship.'

'Hang on,' a twenty-something man in the front interrupted. 'We are only reacting to the pressure our girlfriends are exerting on us. They've all got really fancy ideas these days.'

'That's a valid point,' Clare agreed. 'But, again, it is covering a deeper problem. If your partner is more hung up on how fancy your proposal is than you as a person, I would see that as a red flag in your relationship.'

'Sounds like the idea of marriage is just too hard these days,' the same man said.

'No, it's not,' Clare assured him. 'It's definitely not,' she emphasised. 'You just need to go in better prepared and stop focusing on the wrong things.'

'Hey, Matt,' asked a young man in the middle section. 'You've gotta finish your story, man. Where are you at now? Are you gonna try again?'

Matt shook his head. 'No.'

'So why are you here then?' asked another man from the second row.

Clare looked over at him and raised her eyebrows. 'Yes, that's a good question, gentlemen. But Phil up the front asked a question first, one I'm sure you'd all like the answer to. So, what do you say, Matt, are you going to bring the audience up to speed?'

Matt shook his head. 'No. I think I've said my piece. But you seem to have all the answers, so why don't you finish it off for me?'

'All right, I will.'

* * * * *

As always, Clare's handbag was so full she couldn't close the zip. So even though her phone was on silent, she could see the screen light up when it rang. Determined not to be one of those people who couldn't get through a movie without looking at their mobile, she did her best to ignore the mini disco that was happening at her feet. But when it kept lighting up every minute or so, she had to give in and check.

Lifting her bag onto her knee, Clare slid her phone out and did a double take when she looked at the screen. Thirteen missed calls from Matt! Remembering she was in a crowded movie theatre, she held back from cursing out loud. This was getting ridiculous. She had been resolute in her need to create some distance between them. She needed Matt to realise just how seriously he had stuffed up this time and if she gave in to some drunken, wheedling, sweet talking he would never have any kind of growth experience.

Checking the time on her phone screen, Clare shook her head in annoyance. Nine forty on a Friday night, typical pub time. He was probably absolutely hammered and full of remorse, yet again. Already thoroughly annoyed, she almost exploded when the screen lit up again in her hand.

Right! Clare thought, he's going to get a piece of my mind!

Lifting her thumb to swipe and reject the call she glanced closer at the screen. It was a different number. Knowing she wouldn't be able to get out of her seat fast enough to answer it, Clare had to let it ring out. But she had an uneasy feeling about it that quickly grew when a follow up text message from the same number appeared on her screen seconds later.

"Clare, please call Melanie at the Emergency Department, Royal Brisbane Hospital on this number."

This time Clare's gasp was audible. Jumping to her feet, she jostled her way along the row, ignoring the dirty looks and sighs of annoyance, and ran for the exit.

Clare had to pause then as the audience interrupted with a barrage of questions.

'Hang on a minute,' Phil said. 'Are you saying *you're* the girlfriend?'

Clare nodded, just as Matt said, 'She's actually not my girlfriend anymore.'

'Okay, former girlfriend,' Phil conceded. 'Is this some kind of double act or something?'

'Yeah,' a hefty older man with a buzz cut interjected. 'Why are you giving lectures about the perfect proposal if your bloke messed up so badly?'

Clare held her hand up for order. 'Please, gentlemen, let me finish speaking. I can assure you that Matt was not invited here tonight, however, the fact he is here has given us an opportunity to learn from a real-life case study. If you'll just hear me out, you may find out some pertinent information that may help you avoid what Matt and I experienced.'

'All right,' Phil agreed, 'but if you don't talk sense I want a refund.'

'Yeah,' a few others agreed.

Clare glared over at Matt as if to say, happy now?

He shrugged in return and pulled a face, hoping to get a smile in return.

He didn't.

* * * * *

The Emergency Department waiting room was packed and very noisy. Closest to the front, several people were coughing ferociously, apparently victims of the latest virulent flu strain. A young woman in the middle row held an ice pack against her swollen knee and a middle-aged man, still dressed in his high visibility work gear, cradled a bandaged wrist, apparently in a fair amount of pain. Dozens of other people of all descriptions perched uncomfortably on the remaining hard plastic chairs obviously determined to stay put, despite the sign, which announced the approximate waiting time to be three hours.

Feeling a little guilty for jumping the queue, Clare made her way to the triage window and was immediately buzzed through when she explained who she was. Ignoring the howls of protest that erupted in her wake, she followed Melanie, the nurse who greeted her, in wide-eyed wonder. She had heard about the bedlam in hospital emergency departments on Friday and Saturday nights, but had no idea if it was run of the mill chaos or if there was some kind of major emergency in progress on this particular night. Every cubicle was occupied, and the noise level was high, with the groans of pain, sounds of vomiting and drunken shouting all mingling together. On top of all that were the sounds of the staff as they ministered to their patients and communicated instructions between themselves.

'Can I get some more normal saline in cubicle three?'

'Multi vehicle MVA on the way, we need to clear some beds!'

Melanie shook her head. 'Great! Just what we need on a Friday night.'

Unsure how to respond, Clare just smiled sympathetically and continued to trail her until they reached a cubicle in the farthest corner. Pausing a moment before opening the curtain, Melanie grabbed a clipboard from the wall and handed it to Clare. 'I'll just get you to fill in his admission papers. We're so glad to get hold of you. We tried his mum but she didn't answer and when we asked him he kept saying your name.'

Clare nodded and accepted the forms.

'Sorry, we haven't really had the chance to clean him up yet,' Melanie apologised as she flung the curtain open.

Clare's hand flew to her mouth at the sight that greeted her. Matt was huddled on his side with his knees drawn up, apparently in pain, even though he was sleeping. Vomit stained the front of his navy-blue t-shirt, his khaki cargo shorts were splashed with mud and the soles of his bare feet were filthy. But worse than that was his pallor. His face was a shade of grey that Clare had never seen, and it frightened her. 'Is he drunk?' she asked.

Melanie shook her head. 'No, we thought so at first but it's actually severe food poisoning.'

'Okay, so why is he so dishevelled and shoeless? Where did you find him?'

'He was volunteering at the kids festival at the Ekka grounds this arvo. Apparently he was at the mud pie stand.'

Clare couldn't help but shake her head fondly at her very own Peter Pan. 'Do you know what he ate to cause it?' she asked.

'He said he had leftover Thai takeaway for breakfast, we're assuming it's that.'

Clare rolled her eyes. 'It's probably leftover from a week ago. He's got a theory that as long as there's no mould it's okay to eat.'

'That would probably do it then. Rice in particular can be nasty after a couple of days.'

'Will he be okay?'

'He's been pretty sick, but now we've got the drip in and given him some medication he should start to settle down soon. We'll need to keep him in for at least twelve hours and the drugs we've given him will make him pretty disorientated. Do you want to stay with him?'

'Of course. I can see you guys are totally run off your feet.'

'Yeah, that's pretty much the norm in Emergency. I'll get him cleaned up and into a gown and I can get you a chair, but I'm afraid you may not get too much sleep in here.'

'That's okay.'

'All right, here's the vomit bowl and there's a unisex toilet just down the hallway. He's over the worst of it now, but he'll probably still need to make a trip or two and he's not real steady on his feet.'

Clare took a deep breath. 'All right, no worries.'

Melanie grinned. 'Wow, you're definitely a keeper! I always reckon the true test of a relationship is whether or not a couple will look after each other when they're sick.'

'Well you've got to take the good with the bad.'

'He's a lucky guy,' Melanie replied, smiling again before heading off to find a chair and a gown.

* * * * *

'It's amazing how seeing somebody you love in such a vulnerable position can make everything else seem so unimportant,' Clare said. 'All the anger I'd felt just kind of evaporated and all that mattered was that Matt was going to be okay.'

'So, you're saying you just forgave him for screwing up your career?' Phil asked. Extending his hands to take in their surroundings he said, 'I'm guessing this is a bit of a demotion from the other speaking work you'd been doing.'

Clare shook her head. 'Actually, it's not. Sure, it's not as glamorous and it doesn't pay as much but it is exactly where I want to be.' Looking up at the audience and seeing the evident scepticism she nodded. 'I'm not kidding. You see this situation also forced me to face up to some of *my* own issues.'

'Psychologists have issues?' a man in an Armani suit asked.

'Of course we do, we're human too. I already knew deep down that corporate speaking wasn't my thing. I mean I was good enough at it and it really raised my profile, but it was keeping me away from what I love doing, which is helping people at a grassroots level.'

'So why did you keep doing it?' asked Phil.

Clare shrugged. 'Peer pressure I suppose. All my colleagues seemed to think it was the right path for me to follow and the money was pretty amazing.'

'Then missing your big speech was kind of a blessing in disguise?' asked Armani man.

'Well, yeah. You see, the truth was if I'd really wanted to, I could have still done that speech. I could have tracked the security company down and got them to let somebody into my office and email or fax it to me. I could have even flown back myself and picked it up. It was just more convenient to have the decision taken out of my hands and blame Matt.'

'I did stuff up, though,' said Matt.

'Yeah, but we all do that sometimes. When you love someone, you need to accept them for who they are. I love the way you take life as it comes. And I should have checked you had the USB, in fact knowing the way you lose things I should have put it in my pocket the moment I got in the car.'

'Hang on,' Phil said, looking first at Clare and then at Matt. 'You said you're not together anymore.'

'No, I said she's not my girlfriend,' Matt replied.

'Huh?'

'Okay, enough of the cryptic clues,' Clare said, 'there's a little bit more to the story.'

* * * * *

It was one of the worst nights Clare had ever experienced. Willing herself to be comfortable in the plastic chair but failing miserably, she only managed to nod off for five or ten minutes at a time before being awoken by drunken shouting, Matt's need to throw up (twice) and visit the bathroom (once), several emergency alarms and the general noise of the ED. Still out to it on medication, Matt barely registered her presence beyond giving a woozy smile of recognition.

The arrival of dawn seemed to bring with it a small sense of calm, although Clare was still amazed at the constant level of activity around her. It seemed that people were still violently ill, in pain or suffering heart attacks no matter what the hour. At least Matt was sleeping peacefully now, the combination of fluids and medication obviously having done their job. Although still drawn and pale, his face had lost the awful grey hue.

Just after six, a heavyset older woman poked her head around the curtain. 'Oh, hello, love, I'm just here to mop the floor,' she announced cheerfully. 'Would you mind stepping out for a second?'

Clare stretched and rolled her neck. 'No, that's fine,' she answered wearily, as she stood up and opened the curtain. 'I think I need to go and find some coffee anyway.'

'Good idea I'd say, love. You been here all night, have you?'

'Yeah.'

'Ah, poor thing. He's much better now, though. He was so ill when he first came in.'

'He would have hated that, he's hardly ever sick.'

'Ah, don't worry, he was pretty out of it. I don't think he realised what he was saying. Kept carrying on about his girlfriend and how he—' her voice trailed off and she eyed Clare up and down before saying, 'Are you Clare by any chance?'

'Yes, I am.'

'Oh, right.'

An expert in body language, Clare immediately noticed the change in the woman's demeanour. Those two words conveyed contempt and were a major turnaround from the cheery greeting she had bestowed earlier.

'Is there a problem?' she asked politely.

'No, no problem,' the cleaner replied briskly, as she mopped around the bed.

Clare slipped into professional mode, giving the cleaner a thoughtful, considered stare. 'Are you sure?' she asked in a soft, measured tone.

'Yes!' the cleaner replied, pushing the mop harder as she cleaned the perimeter of the cubicle.

Clare continued to look at the woman, which had the desired effect.

Abandoning her mop and bucket she motioned with her head and directed Clare down the hall a little way.

A little alarmed at this point but not willing to show it, Clare stood and waited expectantly.

'Look, this really isn't my place to say,' the woman began.

'But you're going to anyway.'

'Well, yes, I suppose I am. You young women today, you're just too hard on blokes. They're simple creatures, really, you know. They're not designed to think about things the way women do.'

Sleep deprived, stressed Clare wanted to yell at the woman to mind her own business, but professional Clare realised there was something lurking under the surface. 'Okay, I'll bite, just what are you getting at?'

'Your young man in there, I don't know what you're looking for Clare, but he seems like a decent sort. I can't believe you knocked him back.'

'Knocked him back?' Clare asked, 'knocked him back from what?'

'Oh, come on! The Windsor, your helicopter ride, Centrepoint? What happened at those places?'

'I don't know what you mean. We've never been to The Windsor, the helicopter was fun but uneventful and we had a big fight at Centrepoint.'

The woman paled. 'Really?'

'Yes, really.'

'Oh, oh dear, I think I've got my wires crossed. Yes, yes, I have. I'm thinking of somebody different.'

'No you're not, you're talking about events that involve me.'

The woman sighed. 'You're obviously a smart lady, I think you can join the dots.' And with that she headed back to the cubicle and resumed mopping.

* * * * *

'Now I know why you like *Home and Away*,' Phil interjected. 'You've got the same kind of drama happening in your own life.'

'I don't watch *Home and Away*,' Clare said.

'She totally does,' Matt stage whispered.

'Thanks, Matt, for that wonderful and inaccurate insight, but I think you can take it from here.'

'Okay I will,' he replied with a grin.

* * * * *

Matt knew his face must have registered his confusion as his eyes fluttered open the next morning. It took him a moment to focus, but when he saw Clare sitting by his bedside all other thoughts of where he was and what he was doing fell by the wayside. Although his mouth was dry and pasty and his stomach and head still ached, he couldn't stop the grin that spread across his face.

'Clare,' he murmured.

'Yes,' she replied.

'You're here.'

'Yes.'

'I love you.'

'Yes.'

'Why do you keep saying yes?'

'Because that's my answer.'

'Answer to what?'

'Yes, I'll marry you.'

Matt rubbed sleep from his eyes and tried to focus better. 'What?'

'I said, yes, I'll marry you.'

'But I didn't ask, did I?'

'No, no exactly.'

'Then how did you know?'

'It was something the cleaner said.'

'The cleaner?'

'Long story, but I worked it out. I realised what you've been trying to do.'

'And stuffing up every time.'

'There's no such thing as a stuff up, just another life experience.'

'And I seem to have more of them than average.'

'Oh, Matty, I adore you just as you are and I can't wait to marry you.'

'But that wasn't a proper proposal, I needed it to be perfect.'

'When did I ever say that's what I wanted?'

* * * * *

'So, you got engaged in a hospital emergency department?' asked a bald guy in the fifth row.

'Yep, we did.'

'Wow.'

'Yeah, wow,' Matt agreed. 'After all the effort I'd gone to, all the expense and planning, my fiancée agreed to marry me when I was wearing a hospital gown and had a drip in my arm. I wasn't even wearing my lucky undies.'

Clare shook her head. 'I think that's just a little bit too much information.'

A smattering of laughter broke out.

Matt felt much more relaxed now that the guys were laughing with him and not at him. Still, he couldn't help but add a final chapter to the story.

'Just for the record I did ask her again in a proper setting.'

'Where?' Phil asked.

'On the veranda of the house where we met.'

'And this time it *was* perfect,' Clare said, with the smile that still floored Matt.

'Yep, it was,' he agreed with a grin.

'Okay, so you guys are love's young dream,' Phil said, 'but can you guarantee the same result for us?'

Clare shook her head. 'Of course not, there are no guarantees in life. The main thing I want you to remember is that it doesn't really matter how and where you propose, you should put your focus on a long and committed marriage rather than a fancy engagement. And that means you need to sort out any problems on either side before you take that step. If there are weaknesses or problems in your relationship, proposing won't fix them, it will just mask them for a while. I can guarantee once the honeymoon is over they will surface again with a vengeance.'

'Yeah, but how do we get our girlfriends to understand that?' murmured a thin man with a goatee, sitting in the back section. 'It's no good us getting ourselves sorted if they don't do the same.'

'Tell them to come along to my "Relationships Expectations" course for women,' Clare replied, with a grin.

aving been waylaid by several of the men in the audience, Matt avoided the pack up and was waiting when Clare came out into the foyer.

'You are *so* dead!' Clare said, with her best attempt at a frown. 'I told you not to come, it makes me really nervous.'

'But I missed you.'

'I missed you too, but you could have just gone over to Mum and Dad's and surprised me there.'

'I wanted to see you in action, and I wanted to get some material for the book. If I remember correctly, you did engage my professional services.'

'That would be why you've got a notebook or a recording device with you.'

Matt tapped his temple. 'It's all up here.'

Clare just shook her head and held her arms open. They hugged tightly and kissed passionately, delighted to see one another after so long apart. Clare's touring schedule had been arranged in such a way to get all the presentations done in as short a time as possible, so as to give them more time together in the long run. But the separations were always hard.

Ending the embrace Matt took both Clare's hands in his. 'So,' he said, 'You really do love me just as I am?'

'You know I do.'

'That's a relief because I accidentally left my iPad on the plane and I really want to go and pick it up tonight before it gets lost in the system somewhere. They said they'd keep it at the counter until midnight.'

'Seriously? Driving to the airport at 10:45 pm? You realise how far that is, right?'

'Yeah, sorry.'

Clare shook her head. 'You *are* lucky I love you just as you are,' she said. 'You can drive though,' she added, throwing him the keys.

Matt caught them deftly and depressed the unlock button on the remote. 'No worries, as long as you direct me. I don't know my way from out here.'

Clare shook her head again but couldn't hold back a smile. Opening the back door, she dumped her satchel on the back seat before climbing in the front. After fastening her seatbelt, she extended her left hand and admired the exquisite diamond on the third finger.

Matt fastened his seatbelt and flicked the lights on. 'Nice ring.'

'Yeah, not bad.' Clare replied with a big grin. 'I really like being a fiancée.'

'So do I,' Matt said, leaning in for a kiss.

Clare returned the kiss, then pushed him away playfully. 'Steady on there, mister, we need to make tracks out to Tullamarine.'

'Yeah, all right,' Matt sighed, turning the key in the ignition.

'Okay, head on up to Springvale Road,' Clare said with a yawn.

'Sorry, Hon, but we can sleep in tomorrow and our flight's not until four.'

'Oh, you're on my flight?'

'Of course.'

'Cool, it's always more fun when you're there.'

'Ditto,' Matt said.

'Wow, I can't believe that was the last talk for ages. It will be nice to stay in one place a while.'

'So we'll actually get to see each other every day?'

'You bet and I hope you're prepared, Mr Ryan. We've got a wedding to plan.'

The characters Matt and Clare in The Perfect Proposal first appeared in my novel The Beach House. You can read a preview of it by turning the page.

Prologue

The Sunset Point School of Arts Hall was not used to such commotion. Built in the 1950s, the modest timber structure had hosted Saturday night dances, debutante balls, ballet classes and the local Eisteddfod each year since 1974. Over the years, it had also seen many town meetings, but never one quite like this. All two hundred seats were filled and dozens more people lined the sides and crowded at the back of the hall. A loud buzz of conversation permeated the room. Four people seated at a long table at the front struggled to maintain order and correct meeting procedure.

'Order, please!' Moira Bell said into the microphone. 'Everybody needs to wait their turn to speak.'

When the crowd ignored Moira's request, in fact the noise seemed to increase, Jim Stewart gave a shrill whistle. 'All right!' he shouted. 'Calm down! Mr Walton here has something to say.'

Max Walton stood, but was drowned out before he said his first word.

'Boo! Boo! Boo!' chorused a gang from the back section.

'Greedy land grabber!' bellowed a man in the second row. Heavily built, bearded and dressed in King Gee work clothes, to Max's eye he looked the type who enjoyed this kind of civil protest.

A young woman standing at the side started a chant. 'Go away! Go away! Go away!' It was soon accompanied by rhythmic claps and foot stamping.

Max shook his head, amazed at the ignorance of these people. He wasn't suggesting a Vegas style casino or a brothel, just a luxurious resort.

Reclaiming the microphone, Jim held it near the amplifier, causing an ear-splitting electronic shriek. The hall gradually fell silent. Jim spoke again, now with no need for the microphone. 'We all feel very strongly about this, but in the tradition of a democratic society let Mr Walton speak.'

Max took the microphone again. 'Please just hear what I have to say,' he began, ignoring the few diehards who continued to boo.

Jim held up his hand and the noise trickled to a murmur.

'I know you feel very attached to the beach house and you're right, it is a beautiful building. I want to assure you that it won't be demolished, just moved to another site right here in Sunset Point.'

'Yeah, to a scrubby block near the highway with no view,' said an elderly woman in the front row. Max stared at her in surprise. She looked like such a frail old thing. He was glad her words couldn't be heard over the increasing volume of conversation returning to the room.

Gamely he continued. 'You have to understand; the way it is now it is only accessible to a small group of people each year. With the resort I'm proposing, this wonderful site will be available to hundreds at a time. And don't forget the people staying there don't just spend money on accommodation; they spend it in your shops, your cafe and your cinema. It means your town can expand and grow.'

'We don't want it to grow!' yelled a middle-aged man from the fifth row. 'We like it just as it is! We don't need city problems up here.'

Max shook his head. 'There doesn't have to be city problems. We're talking about modest growth. This is motivated by a genuine desire to help your community.'

The audience erupted again. 'Come off it,' yelled the same man, 'it's motivated by money and greed. We're not just small-town hicks without a clue.'

This time the microphone on the amplifier had no effect

and Max was booed off the stage.

· · · · ·

Two weeks later in the Brisbane office of news magazine *The Queensland Reviewer,* Jessica Stanton sat at her desk admiring the beautiful bouquet of flowers just delivered to her colleague Vanessa. 'You're so lucky Ness,' she said, trying to keep the envy out of her voice. None of her boyfriends had ever done something so romantic for her.

'I told you he was perfect,' Vanessa said as she inhaled the scent of the pink and white roses. Picking up the florist's card, she read aloud, 'Budding Blooms. Hmm, I'd heard they do fabulous arrangements. Weren't they mentioned in a story we did recently?'

Jessica nodded. 'Yeah, it was one of mine. They did the flowers for that society wedding, you know Amanda McMillan-Byrne and William Ashton?'

'Oh yeah. It was at Mt Tamborine, right?'

'Uh huh. The bouquets and centrepieces from Budding Blooms were so exquisite that I interviewed the florist as well and did an extra piece about her.'

'I don't remember reading it.'

'Grant hasn't run it yet,' Jessica said.

'Well, I think I'll keep their card. I might need their services in the not-too-distant future.' Vanessa smiled dreamily as she reached for the vase on top of the filing cabinet.

Rolling her eyes, Jessica turned her attention to the memo the editor-in-chief Grant Morris had deposited in her in-tray ten minutes earlier. It was her new story assignment: *Landmark legal case in the works for small coastal village of Sunset Point.*

Jessica sighed inwardly as she eyed off the attached pile of printed pages. Grant loved extensive background information and he always questioned his staff to make sure they'd actually read it.

With nothing else pressing to finish for the day, Jessica decided to make a start on it before heading over to Indooroopilly. It was late-night shopping and she'd arranged to meet her sister so they could buy their mother's birthday present.

Turning off her computer to avoid distractions, Jessica leaned back in her chair and began to read the background synopsis.

Sunset Point is a small town on an undeveloped section of the central Queensland coastline. Featuring a popular swimming and surfing beach, the town, with a permanent population of around three thousand, is flooded with holiday makers during the summer months and school holiday periods. A beachfront caravan park/campground and several small beach shacks cater for holiday visitors.

The other landmark of Sunset Point is a heritage-listed Queenslander known locally as "The Beach House". Set on what is considered to be the finest piece of land in the town, it was built almost 100 years ago by Clem McMaster, a local sawmill worker, after winning the lottery.

Jessica paused in her reading and studied the exterior photos of the house. It was indeed a beautiful old building. She could imagine holidaymakers relaxing on the veranda enjoying the cool beach vibe while their beach towels hung drying on the wooden railings.

I haven't been to the beach in ages, she thought. I might

head down to the Gold Coast this weekend. It's still too cold to swim but I'll go early and have a nice walk and … Realising she was daydreaming, she shook her head and turned her attention back to the pages in her hand.

Clem's eldest son Richard inherited the house and initially it was a private holiday retreat but was later converted into an exclusive health resort. On Richard's death, ownership of the house passed on to his only son James, a man of vision who was cynical about the class structure that still existed in twentieth century society. Although born into wealth – thanks to his grandfather's careful investments – James felt restricted by wealth and the associated expectations of society. Determined that the beach house would not be an exclusive domain of the wealthy, James opened it up as a regular holiday rental.

Glancing at her watch, Jessica noticed it was almost five o'clock. Her workmates were starting to pack up, including Vanessa with her huge bunch of flowers. She should get going too. But now she was this far into her reading, she may as well finish before she left. Waving goodbye to her colleagues, she slid off the uncomfortable shoes she'd been trying to wear in for the past week and continued reading.

Critical of the trappings of the modern world, the only conveniences James allowed in the house were a radio and a telephone, ruling that no television was ever to be installed. Further clauses were added by the Beach House committee (see note below) as technology developed to also prohibit the internet and any electronic devices.

James never married nor had any children, so he willed the house to the town of Sunset Point. However, in order to maintain ownership, the house could never be sold or removed from the site, nor the land subdivided. The aforementioned conditions instigated by James also needed to remain intact. The rental income from the property was to be divided among approved local charities. A management committee, with strictly regulated membership, was formed to oversee the house and to ensure that James's wishes were upheld.

Jessica turned the page but the back of the paper was blank. Annoyed, she shuffled through the pages in her In tray, but the rest of the information wasn't there either. Knowing Grant would still be in his office, she made her way down the hall.

Looking up when Jessica appeared at his door, Grant checked his watch and shot her a quizzical glance.

'Yes, I know, it's after five and I'm still here. That deserves some brownie points, doesn't it?' Jessica smiled hopefully.

Grant shrugged. 'I guess so. You came down just to tell me that?'

'Of course not. That background info you gave me about the beach house story, there's some pages missing.'

'I'm still reading it myself,' Grant said, holding up a few sheets of paper. 'I figured I had at least until tomorrow before you got around to reading the first part.'

Jessica came in and sat down. 'I had a few spare minutes so I thought I'd get started on it today and I hate leaving things half-read. I'm just up to the part about the committee.'

'Intriguing story, isn't it? Not your average small-town-versus-developer scenario.' Grant raised an eyebrow and leaned back in his chair.

'No, it's way more than that. But you left me hanging. What happened with the committee?'

'Well, the committee, a group of upstanding local citizens, has done its job excellently for the past twenty-five years without any problem. The community is happy, the people who stay in the house are happy.'

'What's the angle, then? How can the developer even mount a court case?'

'Ah, this is where it gets a bit murky. Their local council was amalgamated two years ago. So now their former mayor, who is very conservative, is just one of fourteen councillors on a much larger regional council. And the new mayor is very pro-development.'

'What about the heritage listing?'

'Well, because he's promising to move the building fully intact to another site in the same area, it's not an issue.'

'How did this Max guy even find out about the house?'

'His car broke down and he spent two days in Sunset Point waiting for a new head gasket. Apparently, he did some exploring and cast his developer's eye over the house site and adjoining blocks. His expensive legal team then found him a loophole in the regulations – the local council, which is now the regional council, has the discretion to modify the ownership clause in extraordinary circumstances.'

'How is this extraordinary?'

'Two of the amalgamated shires had major debt and one of the former mayors was deposed for embezzlement just before the election. The sale of this land would make a fair hole in their budget deficit.'

'What about the adjoining blocks? Can't he buy them instead?'

'Yes, possibly, but they aren't worth much without the beach house site. It's got the access and the beach frontage.

This resort he's planning is huge and he needs all the land.'

'So now it's going to court and you want me to follow the case?' Jessica asked, her eyes lighting up at the prospect of her by-line appearing on something that was sure to capture a lot of public attention. *This* was the kind of story that could get her noticed. After almost a year working here, Grant was finally giving her something exciting to write about.

Grant held his hand up in a calming gesture. 'Hang on there, Jess. Yes, you can do the court case, but I want to set the scene first. We ran a brief filler piece last fortnight that also ran in the New South Wales and Victorian editions. I've had a stack of emails, letters and phone calls from people who've stayed there and they've all got a story to tell. So, I want you to interview five of them and see what comes up. They're all surprisingly passionate about saving the house.'

Jessica reached over and took the pile of printed pages from Grant. She stood up but paused before leaving. 'I get how they can block the internet by not having any kind of modem or wireless set up in the house, but how can you stop people taking their gadgets with them?'

'Ah, young Gen-Y Jessica, we can survive without technology you know,' Grant said with a smile. 'Apparently, they use the old-fashioned honour system. Obviously they can't search people's belongings but each tenant is asked not to bring those items and, on arrival, the real estate agent reminds them again of the house rules. Maybe it's like the old adage, if you do cheat then you're only cheating yourself.'

Jessica, who was very attached to her own gadgets, raised her eyebrows. 'How so?'

'Read the emails and my phone call summaries and you'll start to understand.'

Jessica took the pages back to her desk but set them aside. She would humour Grant and do the human-interest stories, but her first priority was getting some background information on Max Walton. Then, when she wrote about the court case, the thoroughness of her research skills would be evident. That was the kind of thing major daily newspaper editors looked for in their staff.

Turning her computer back on, Jessica logged onto the internet and googled "Malton Construction and Development". Scrolling through the numerous pages returned by the search, she felt a frisson of excitement. This thing was going to be *big*. Max Walton was a heavyweight in coastal development and he wasn't afraid of controversy. He'd already won two lawsuits against local governments that had tried to block his construction projects in their areas.

Clicking on a link Jessica looked at a photograph of Malton's newest resort in Western Australia. It was magnificent but, according to the caption, not entirely welcome. Apparently the town of Moon Bay had also been divided about whether it should go ahead. Jessica scribbled the name in her notebook. She'd have to find out what their local paper was called and look up some story clips. Hopefully it would give her some ideas.

Grant stopped at Jessica's cubicle at six thirty, carrying his briefcase. Totally engrossed in an article about Max's last court case, she jumped in fright when he spoke.

'Jess, you know I love a dedicated worker but I don't want you walking to your car in the dark by yourself.'

Jessica bookmarked the web page and hit the hibernate key. 'Yes, I know, safety first. In any case, I'm supposed to be at Indro now, selecting my mother's birthday gift. My sister will kill me for being late.'

Grant held the back door open and Jessica walked past

him into the almost empty car park. Waiting while she unlocked her car, Grant checked his phone. 'My wife just texted me to say that if I wasn't home in twenty minutes, the dog is getting my dinner,' he said, sliding his Blackberry into his back pocket.

'I hope the traffic's not too bad then.' Jessica grinned as she threw her bag on the passenger seat.

'Me too. If that mutt gets lasagne and I'm stuck with beans on toast I won't be very happy.'

Jessica paused for a moment, standing between the open car door and the driver's seat. 'Thanks for walking me out. You get here about seven most mornings, don't you?'

'I do indeed, sometimes a bit earlier when we're on deadline. Should I expect to see you here early too tomorrow?'

Jessica nodded. 'I can't wait to get started.'

• • • • •

Almost a week later, Jessica finalised her list of interviewees. It had taken longer than planned to sift through the emails and call summaries to determine which ones to use. Frankly she thought Grant was putting too much emphasis on this angle, rather than backgrounding Max Walton and his development empire, but she had to keep him sweet or he might put someone more experienced on the court case.

Just play by the rules Jessica, she kept reminding herself.

Sitting in Grant's office later, she tapped her foot on the carpeted floor, as he examined the list. Grant had the ability to read through information without showing any change in facial expression, so Jessica had no idea what he was thinking. Eventually he looked up and nodded.

'Good work, Jess. I like the mix of backgrounds and it's a nice even timeline.'

'Well, that just kind of fell into place. I wasn't really aiming for any particular era. But I think it would be good if we ran them in sequence.'

'Yes, I agree,' said Grant. 'But what about the interstate ones? Phone interviews? Or are you going to Skype them?' Grant had no problems with using technology, but he did think that sometimes the younger staff relied on it too much, rather than developing more intuitive journalistic skills.

'No, it's all old school, face to face, and it's not costing you much at all. I managed to work them into my Melbourne trip.'

'Trip?'

Jessica swallowed her impatience. 'I'm going to Melbourne for a wedding. Remember, I asked you for next Friday off? I'll need the Monday and Tuesday too, now, so I can come back via Sydney.'

'Right, right, sure, I remember and yes, you can take the extra days. That's good if you can do it that way.' Grant eyed his newest reporter. 'This is a pretty big task, Jess. Are you sure you're up to it? We can divide the interviews up, if you want.'

Jessica shook her head. There was no way she was letting anyone muscle in on this assignment and potentially steal the story of the year. 'No, it's totally fine. I don't mind doing some extra hours.'

'All right, then. I must say, I'm glad that you seem to have lost your aversion to human interest stories. Like I've told you numerous times already, journalism is not always about the big headlines.'

Jessica smiled benignly, desperately hoping she looked sincere. 'What can I say? You're right again, boss.'

KATE — 1991

Kate Green added another fancy swirl to the elaborate doodle she was creating in her notebook. It was one of her best yet, taking up almost half a page. Turning the book on its side she was eyeing her work of art critically when she heard her name called. Flinching, she cast her eyes to the front of the classroom, mortified to have been caught daydreaming.

The blackboard was covered in writing and diagrams, but gave no real clue of the question she had just been asked.

Kate opened her mouth to respond, but then noticed other students returning to their seats holding papers and realised the lecturer was handing back their last assignment. Breathing a sigh of relief, she slunk down to the front desk, keeping her eyes downcast as she grabbed her assignment from the pile so as to avoid the stern gaze of Associate Professor Harold Frezwar.

A tall, rotund, balding man who habitually wore a starched white shirt and a tie, Harold Frezwar lived and breathed economics and expected the same enthusiasm from his students. Considering she had *zero* passion for the subject, theirs was not a very warm affiliation.

Kate's heart began to pound as she made her way back to her seat. I'm sure I've failed, she thought grimly. I threw this together at the very last moment with only the vaguest understanding of the subject matter. Harold is such a hard marker, there's no way he would have passed it.

Sitting back down, Kate put her assignment on the desk but couldn't bring herself to flip it over and read her grade on the back. She had hoped for another few days of grace before this particular nightmare came back to haunt her.

Harold's voice broke into her thoughts. 'All in all, the standard of the essays was reasonable,' he intoned. 'Although, of course, there were several that I simply could not pass.' Pausing dramatically, he cast his unyielding gaze around the room, settling, it seemed, right on Kate.

Heat suffused her neck and face. Just get it over with, she thought. Open the stupid thing and see how badly you actually did. Taking a deep breath, she turned the stack of pages over to reveal the grading sheet with her mark written boldly in red.

53%.

Kate stared at the numbers for a moment, certain she must be seeing things. She had passed! Just barely, but it was enough. Exhaling sharply, she smiled in relief. Somehow, she had scraped through again, but, at the same time, she knew her luck couldn't hold out forever. At some point she was going to have to shake off this apathy.

Noticing the time, Kate packed up her belongings and as soon as Harold dismissed the class, she bolted out the door.

It was a hot October day. Kate fanned herself with a notebook as she sat near the main entrance to Queensland University of Technology, sweltering in the midday sun. Checking her watch, she sighed impatiently. Her friend Fiona was always late. Even when she gave a fake meeting time quarter of an hour earlier than the actual time, Fiona never showed up first.

Ten minutes later Fiona finally emerged. She jostled her way through the crowds of students milling around the campus entrance and jogged towards Kate. Why does she bother rushing now? wondered Kate, as she stood and slung her backpack over her shoulder. She's already this late, what's another minute?

'Sorry, sorry,' Fiona said, as she bustled over. 'The queue for the photocopier was huge and then I couldn't find my library card. I had to unpack my whole purse, then I realised it was in my pocket all along.'

Kate nodded. At least her excuses were original. She rarely used the same one twice.

'How come we're meeting this early, anyway?' Fiona asked, as she unscrewed the lid off her water bottle. 'Didn't you have that tute for accounting?'

'Nah, decided to ditch it.'

'Well, shopping is definitely more exciting,' Fiona said before taking a swig of water. 'And you've gotta love the fact that the Queen Street Mall is right on our doorstep.'

'Absolutely,' Kate agreed.

It was late afternoon when they disembarked from the bus, each holding a shopping bag. 'Are you sure your mum doesn't mind me coming over for dinner again?' Kate asked.

'Nah, she sees it as her civic duty to ensure you get a home cooked meal as often as possible.'

They both laughed.

A carpet of jacaranda blooms littered the nature strip in Fiona's street. 'They're so pretty,' Kate said, as they sloughed through them. 'And they make you realise summer is not far away.'

'Yeah, but watch your head,' Fiona advised.

'What?'

'Haven't you heard the University of Queensland legend that if a bloom falls on your head during exam time then you're destined to fail?'

Kate leapt back onto the bitumen and cast a fearful eye up at the tree, lest a whole branch come crashing down on her. Then she laughed. 'We don't even go to UQ and exams are still ages away.'

• • • • •

Even with the end of the semester looming, The Victory pub

was packed on Saturday night two weeks later. Happy hour was in full swing and Kate was relieved to see that she and her friends weren't the only ones who had ditched studying for the night.

'Mel and her friends are working on some group assignment,' she yelled in Fiona's ear. 'So it's not like I'd be able to study anyway with them all there.'

Hiking up her precarious strapless top Fiona gave a wry smile. 'Yeah, how inconsiderate,' she yelled back. 'Forcing you to go out and party instead.'

Kate poked out her tongue. Fiona grinned in reply as she adjusted her top again.

Fixing a carefree expression on her face Kate sipped her West Coast Cooler and bopped along to Hunters and Collectors. Fiona was *so* lucky she could get away with such a revealing outfit. Her own top was much more sedate. No matter what they said about black being slimming, it was difficult to disguise the eight extra kilos she had gained this year. She wasn't overweight exactly, but not slender anymore either. It was something she had always taken for granted before.

Fiona leaned over to shout in Kate's ear again. 'Are you going to stay sharing with Mel next year?'

Rolling her eyes dramatically, Kate shrugged. 'Who knows? Anyway, I might not even be here next year.'

Placing her empty glass on a table, Fiona grabbed Kate's wrist. 'You're not really thinking about leaving, are you?'

Sighing, Kate shrugged again. 'I don't know! I just can't stand the thought of studying business for another two whole years.'

'Then change courses. You're getting good at that,' Fiona smirked.

'I know, I know, all the chopping and changing has been

157

a bit ridiculous – but I really wanted to do criminal psychology. I can't believe they rejected me.'

'Well they're a bit of a snobby bunch at SEQU,' Fiona said, pronouncing it *SeeKwoo* rather than by its initials. 'Would you really want to go there?'

'Yes, I would, I really had my heart set on it. Two more years is such a long time to endure economics and accounting.'

Fiona adjusted her top again. 'Yeah, maybe, but think of the partying you'll miss if you leave. Come on, Kate, nobody enjoys studying, it's the lifestyle we're here for. We've got two more years to have fun, enjoy long holidays and make the most of being young and carefree. Then when we're finished we can bum around Europe for a year or something.'

Kate took her last mouthful of West Coast and set the bottle on the table. 'Fine, I'll think about it.'

'I know you, Kate – the minute you have to start writing job applications, you'll cut your losses and decide to stay.'

Early the next afternoon Kate stared glassy eyed at the cars hurtling around the racetrack. I'm really scraping the bottom of the barrel, she decided as she lay listlessly on the couch. Motor racing is the watching paint dry of weekend TV and I'm using it as a distraction.

Hauling herself to her feet a few minutes later, she flicked the TV off before gathering the various sections of *The Sunday Mail* into a semi-neat pile. Salvaging the sealed hand wipe and extra napkin from the KFC box, Kate dumped them in the junk basket on the kitchen bench before heading to her room.

Finally seated at her desk, Kate ploughed through her economics questions. Frustrated to know so few of the answers, she started doodling. WHO CARES??? she scrawled under question five. Well, it was lucky that some people *did* care, or else the world economy would be in lots of trouble. It wasn't that she didn't see the point of economics, she had just realised early on that it wasn't something she wanted to spend time thinking about.

Eventually tossing the worksheet aside, she moved on to accounting. No more appealing than economics, Kate struggled to stay focused once again. Having missed tutorials for the past three weeks, she cursed her own laziness. She would definitely attend tomorrow and round up notes from someone.

At eight thirty Kate shuffled out to the kitchen in search of something to eat. While Mel's shelves held a reasonable stockpile of food, hers were depressingly empty. Even if she had the energy to go out in search of take-away, her options at this time on a Sunday night were limited. And she wasn't quite desperate enough to risk eating a hot dog from the servo down the road.

Making a face, Kate grabbed her last can of baked beans and stole a slice of Mel's bread to make toast. Upending the beans into a bowl, she stuck it in the microwave and set the timer.

Nothing happened.

'No, don't do this now,' she cried, giving the console a well-practised thump.

Still nothing.

I've had it with this stupid thing, Kate fumed, banging her hand down on top of it. This time she was rewarded with a welcome hum.

As the beans spun around slowly, she clicked the TV on. I'll just watch while I eat, she reasoned. Then I'll get back to it.

Beans and toast in hand Kate plonked onto the couch and

channel surfed for a few moments, eager for any diversion from uni work. She found it in *Back To The Future*. 'Cool!' she exclaimed, happy to have stumbled across one of her favourite movies.

Having seen the movie countless times on video, Kate decided she would only watch until nine thirty. But inevitably that deadline came and went. At ten o'clock she conceded it was too late to start studying again and instead kept watching until the credits rolled. As she collapsed into bed at ten forty-five, Kate promised herself that this coming week she would *really* get motivated.

· · · · ·

Five days later, Kate took in the familiar surrounds of her guidance counsellor's office, before glancing again at the commemorative World Expo '88 clock on the wall. The secretary had shown her in and assured her that Patricia was coming, but it was now nine thirty and her appointment had been for twenty past. Like Fiona, Patricia always seemed to be running late.

When she finally bustled in, Kate was sure she caught a hint of impatience in her greeting. 'Kate, hello... again,' she murmured, dumping a pile of folders on an already overloaded desk.

A short, plump woman with steel grey hair, Patricia always looked a little harassed. Or maybe it's just in my presence, Kate thought. I must be one of the ficklest students she has ever come across.

'So, what can I do for you today?' Patricia asked, lowering herself carefully onto her bright pink swivel chair.

'I'm just letting you know I'll soon be out of your hair,' Kate said. 'I'm going to withdraw.'

Patricia's face softened. 'Well, we did talk about that. I think taking a year out would be a really good thing for you. It will give you a chance to work out what you really want to do. And you'll have this year's credit to use as a building block for something else. Just let them know at admin.'

'No, I mean I'm withdrawing now. As of today.'

Patricia's jaw dropped. 'What on earth for? There's only one week until study break.'

'I've had enough. All week I've been sitting in lectures and tutes gradually coming to the realisation there's no way I can catch up. What's the point in sitting exams I'm going to fail?'

'But you'll get four fails on your transcript anyway if you withdraw now. If you at least try, you might make a conceded pass or even a pass. It will give you lots more options.'

'No, my mind is made up,' Kate assured her. 'Not getting into criminal psychology was obviously a sign. I'm just not meant to be at university. Thanks for all your help anyway.' Kate smiled as she stood to leave, revelling in the sense of relief her decision had brought about.

Patricia stood too. 'Oh Kate, I wish you wouldn't. Please think about this more! At the very least don't officially drop out yet. I'd hate you to change your mind.'

Kate shook her head as she walked to the door. 'Trust me, I won't.'

• • • • •

Kate sat up straight and peered out the window at the green road sign in the distance. Could it actually be…? Yes, it was! Sunset Point 10km. She sighed in relief. Long bus journeys were such a bore and thanks to road works on the two-lane highway, this one had turned into a marathon.

She couldn't believe she was doing this. Reaching into her

backpack Kate pulled out the letter and read it again.

Dear Miss Green,

We are pleased to advise that your application to enrol in the Bachelor of Criminal Psychology course has been tentatively approved. Once we have been officially advised of your successful completion of this semester's units with a GPA of at least 4.5, you will be sent the next part of the application pack. Please note that any fail grades on your academic transcript will disqualify you from entry to this program. Furthermore, should you not accept this position you will not be eligible to reapply for three years.

Yours truly,
Sarah Lowes
Assistant Dean, Department of Psychology
South-East QLD University

It had taken a lot of convincing, on both Patricia and her mother's behalf, before Kate decided to give her exams one more shot. As Patricia had pointed out, she had managed to bluff her way through the year without much effort and she had a favourable exam timetable, with her first exam five days in. If she really put her mind to it, maybe she could pull it off.

Twenty minutes later, Kate watched idly as the driver unloaded the luggage, not minding that hers was the last to come off. Anything that delayed the reality of serious study was welcome at this point.

Dragging her bag behind her, Kate hailed the lone taxi waiting nearby. The house wasn't far away but her bag was full of textbooks and way too heavy to carry any distance.

'Whew,' the taxi driver said, putting it in the boot. 'Are you building a house with those bricks?'

Kate smiled politely but didn't encourage any conversation. She was lost in thought as the car made its short journey towards Blue Pacific Boulevard, summing up in her mind the pros of coming to a beach house to study. Firstly, getting away from people and things that could distract her made sense. Secondly, there wasn't even a TV in the house. Thirdly, she'd always found the beach to be very relaxing. Maybe being close to the ocean would help her really focus.

The driver carried her bag up onto the veranda. Kate handed him a ten-dollar note and told him to keep the change.

'No, love, I couldn't,' he said, handing her back some dollar coins.

He gave a friendly wave as he drove away and Kate hoped that such a positive start to her time here was a good omen.

The Beach House is available in paperback and as an e-book.

OTHER BOOKS BY HELEN MCKENNA

Room 46

At first glance, there is nothing special about Room 46. Yet once people step across the threshold, unexpected things start to happen.

Grace has been hiding in a cocoon, convinced that the life she once imagined for herself is now unattainable. But from the first time she reluctantly knocks on the door and enters Room 46, her days of retreating from the world are numbered.

Despite inspiring others on a daily basis, Edith continues to be defined by her tragic past. Can her time in Room 46 help her gain the courage to simply be herself again and to live a full life?

And Marion – what's her story and why is she so invested in what happens in Room 46?

Little does each woman know the hand fate has played in bringing them to this special place to transform their lives in ways they can't imagine.

Third Offence

To Jack Nolan, young Danny is like a son. Despite Danny's rough start in life, Jack saw potential in the boy that few others did and encouraged Danny to pursue dreams he never imagined he could achieve.

But an anonymous letter about his long absent father makes Danny question everything. Can he really rise about his background or is his future set in stone?

Jack is a lawyer at the top of his game and there is nothing he wouldn't do for Danny, who helped him many years ago, as a mere child. But the more Jack uncovers, the more he sees his chances of winning his first criminal case slipping through his fingers.

With time and mounting evidence stacked against them, Jack and Danny negotiate a web of lies and deception, Danny's dread that history will repeat itself and Jack's fear that he is in way over his head. Can they actually uncover the truth and, more importantly, will their friendship survive the ordeal?

Third Offence is also a sequel story to The Beach House.

ABOUT THE AUTHOR

Helen McKenna lives on the Sunshine Coast in Queensland, Australia. She has a Bachelor of Arts degree from the University of Queensland and has worked in banking, local government and as a biographer. As well as writing, she currently works in learning support and as a swimming teacher.

Helen loves to hear from her readers, so please feel free to drop her a line:

Email: info@helenmckenna.com.au
Website: www.helenmckenna.com.au
Facebook: www.facebook.com/HelenMcKenna.Author
Twitter: www.twitter.com/helenmckenna

All paperbacks are currently available directly from her website and from Amazon and all titles are also available as e-books at the major retailers.